GERALD MOORE was born in Hertfordshire in 1899 but spent many of his early years in Canada. He studied at the Toronto School of Music, intending to take up a career as a solo pianist. On his return to London he was advised by Sir Landon Ronald, who heard him play for a young singer, that accompanying was the course he should take. And so he did, becoming internationally known not just as the most distinguished exponent of the accompanist's art, but also as wit, raconteur, lecturer and writer. He played for such renowned figures as Chaliapin, Elena Gerhardt, Hans Hotter, Elisabeth Schumann, Eva Turner, Kathleen Ferrier, John McCormack and Pablo Casals, and, in more recent years, for Janet Baker, Elisabeth Söderström, Yehudi Menuhin, Nicolai Gedda and Jacqueline du Pré. His farewell concert at the Royal Festival Hall in February 1967 has become a legend and a cherished memory for all who were there: on this occasion three singers closely associated with Gerald Moore – Dietrich Fischer-Dieskau, Elisabeth Schwarzkopf and Victoria de los Angeles – joined forces to pay tribute to him in a concert devised by Walter Legge. (Most of that concert can be heard on an EMI compact disc entitled *Gerald Moore: A Tribute*.)

Gerald Moore published a number of successful books, including his autobiographical memoirs *Am I Too Loud?*, *Farewell Recital* and *Furthermoore* (Hamish Hamilton and Penguin Books); studies of the songs of Schubert and Schumann; and *Singer and Accompanist* (Hamish Hamilton). This illustrated edition of his most famous and enduring book, *The Unashamed Accompanist*, contains new material specially written by the distinguished accompanists Geoffrey Parsons and Graham Johnson.

After his retirement Gerald Moore lived quietly in Buckinghamshire with his wife Enid, whom he often described as "the perfect accompanist". He died in 1987.

GERALD MOORE

The Unashamed Accompanist

WITH A FOREWORD BY GEOFFREY PARSONS
AND AN AFTERWORD BY
GRAHAM JOHNSON

Julia MacRae Books

A DIVISION OF WALKER BOOKS

This edition © 1984 Gerald Moore
Foreword © 1984 Geoffrey Parsons
Afterword © 1984 Graham Johnson
All rights reserved
The Unashamed Accompanist was first published in 1943
This revised edition first published in Great Britain 1984 by
Julia MacRae Books, a division of Walker Books Ltd
87 Vauxhall Walk
London SE11 5HJ
Paperback edition first published 1990

Printed and bound in Great Britain by
Butler & Tanner Ltd, Frome and London

Designed by Douglas Martin

The jacket photograph, © 1990 Mike Galletly,
incorporates a photograph of Gerald Moore by Godfrey Argent

British Library Cataloguing in Publication Data
Moore, Gerald, *1899–1987*
The unashamed accompanist. –Rev.ed.
1. Music. Accompaniment: Piano playing. Moore, Gerald,
1899–1987
I. Title
786.2092

ISBN 0-86203-496-5

Contents

The Gerald Moore Award

In January 1991, The Gerald Moore Award
is to be inaugurated. It will be awarded annually
to a young accompanist.
Details and conditions for entry should be available
from colleges of music.

Illustrations

Foreword

IN SPITE OF WAR, this wonderful book made its way to my native Australia soon after its publication in 1943. I came upon it in the library of the Conservatorium of Music in Sydney where I had just become a part-time student. I remember devouring it almost at one gulp, recognising the musical qualities I was already being taught and experiencing as a solo piano student, which its author extolled as being necessary as well for an accompanist. I recall too my excitement as I saw that it was possible, on the other side of the world at any rate, to consider accompanying as a way to make one's life in music, indeed to make a living, and even a respected – and respectable – one. Even then somewhere in my mind was the idea of becoming an accompanist, arising initially perhaps from the example set by a friend of my parents', who was Sydney's best known accompanist and the only professional musician I knew. This role he combined with the roles of singing teacher, coach, choral conductor and organist, however, and I hadn't realised until *The Unashamed Accompanist* appeared that it was possible to be an accompanist *without* the combined exercise of all those other talents as well. The name of Gerald Moore was for me one of the best known of all musicians, for even as a child I was an indefatigable listener to records played on the wireless, and it seemed to me then that Gerald Moore was the accompanist on every second one. This I later discovered to be true! Many of those records I used to hear are now difficult to find, but when I hear one again, like Gerald Moore accompanying Marta Fuchs in "Storchenbotschaft", Nancy Evans in Warlock's "Consider", or the "Arpeggione" with Feuermann, I feel not only admiration but also that same anticipatory thrill I used in my youth to experience at the thought that I, too, might one day be working in such a way.

The Unashamed Accompanist made me aware that this might become a real possibility. It guides, it expounds, it warns, it encourages, and, not only incidentally, it amuses – all of this coming from a fund of experience and wisdom, belying the fact that its author then boasted fewer years than have elapsed since the book's publication. In this time there has been no need, from the point of view of this accompanist at any rate, to alter anything in it. Indeed it is marvellous to have the book again available, not only to us accompanists to whom it must always rank among the permitted Desert Island Books with the Bible and Shakespeare, but to a younger generation of accompanists – budding, successful, amateur or professional – as well as audiences, agents, impresarios, entrepreneurs and, yes, musical colleagues, some of whom may have the occasional lapse in their understanding of what an accompanist does, should do, hopes to be allowed to do, is required to do by the composer, and should be paid for it! (Here I momentarily relinquish my association with Moore's mandatory mercenary modesty!)

In 1982 I accepted an idea proposed by the Barbican Centre in London to arrange a series of song recitals for its opening season. The programme for each of these recitals included a small article on what I believe to be the role of the accompanist, which the management thought might make the audience more aware of what they were hearing from the *accompanist* as well as from the singer, since in this case, very unusually, the accompanist was responsible for the putting together of the series.

I began this article by asserting that primarily the accompanist had to have the musical qualities required by all performers – rhythm, line, shape, style and so on – and continued: "The accompanist has to hold his convictions about them and the expressive content of the music as strongly as the next man." The worst thing an accompanist can be is a piece of blotting paper, soaking up, even musically, the convictions or ideas of his partner without demur.

This boundless will to please is misguided and can only end in a performance lacking the essential tension of two artists striving, in their *own* ways, for the same goal. Adaptability or flexibility is required of an accompanist to an almost infinite extent – "never losing sight of his convictions and his duty as he sees it to the composer – and the poet – while simultaneously and sensitively respecting the viewpoint of his co-interpreters, different as they are and each of whom has his conviction" – here I wrote in my article "not less valid", but perhaps I could also say "more or less valid", depending on a partner's talent, experience and integrity. It actually does happen that in a song where the poetic and musical ideas are paramount, the singer sings with an eye only to its vocal effect and the gallery! Such a viewpoint in such a song I find hard to respect, though in appropriate music there's no one who will more happily help someone to rise to a vocal climax than I.

How wonderful it is to have those artists in whom vocal beauty and interpretative power are equally matched, and presented with equal enthusiasm – with such artists one is most happily adaptable, for spontaneous inspiration, a moment of new insight which produces an unrehearsed nuance or expression, arouses new possibilities of adaptation in the accompanist, so that together Parnassus is momentarily attained – or its green wooded slopes at any rate. It's also possible for the accompanist to initiate this journey to the heights, and then the singer has the job, and the joy, of adapting. These moments of magic are unforgettable for the performers, and audiences are aware of artistic horizons suddenly becoming limitless. Alas, they are rare and virtually unrepeatable – we would love them to linger, to grasp them, but it is in the nature of a performer's life that they are transitory, nevertheless we feel them as the highest rewards.

There are also artists, capable of rising to these heights, who are not concerned with adapting to any ideas outside their own. I recall one singer, rightly very highly respected by the public and her colleagues (not necessarily a usual combination) and by me. When I asked if she preferred the introduction to a certain song played like this . . . or like this . . .? she replied: "It is of absolutely no importance to me *how* you play it"! I have accompanied her at some memorable recitals, which perhaps says something for the possibility of achieving artistic unity from two valid convictions combining, with a very effective though tacit adaptability on the part of both singer and accompanist. The ability to adapt to any given circumstance in music or any created by a singer comes from the most sensitive and active listening. In performance one is ALL antennae, prepared at any moment to continue to recreate the music, albeit sometimes anew (even if from ashes suddenly blackened), a warmth, an atmosphere, a colour, a shape, from what one has just heard, however remote from what was rehearsed. Perhaps the things that identify a real accompanist are his ears, and the way his artistic imagination causes him to react to what they tell him.

Adaptability must be possible on another plane and another scale. Of course accompanists play for many singers – and instrumentalists – and each of these, as I have said, has his or her approach to the music. "Gretchen am Spinnrade", for instance, can be faster or slower, younger or older sounding, passionate or hysterical, louder or softer, to say nothing of higher or lower, and we accompanists have to make her sound as spontaneous and natural as *we* believe Schubert saw her, at the same time never losing sight of this particular singer's point of view and/or possibilities, and the difference between singers' interpretations of the songs – sometimes on consecutive nights with different artists. All this can confuse all but the most convinced and aware, and may lead to a sort of "accompanist's identity crisis" wherein one can almost adapt oneself into forgetting one's own beliefs. This malaise is most strenuously to be resisted – non-resistance can only lead to the ranks in the blotting-paper brigade, and bland uncommitted blanket versions of songs which will more or less do for everyone. The last word about adaptability is in this book: "*At the performance* (my italics) he must be *with* the singer but afterwards let him erase the memory of it from his mind so that the next time he tackles this piece of music his playing will not be tainted by this so-called interpretation."

Accompanists need not necessarily be virtuosi (*pace* Richter,

Brendel, Barenboim, etc – and thanks!), but we have to possess resources of technique which can be dipped into to provide the brilliance of execution required by "Feuerreiter", "Erlkönig", "Aufträge" and many other songs. We may have to practise them more than a virtuoso might, but we can achieve a comparable insight into the technical requirements of a song and bring it off as the composer wanted. We also hope, as always, to have pleased our singer colleague as well.

But brilliance is perhaps the least required technical attribute for an accompanist – the most is a supportive and, almost always, a beautiful tone. This tone quality has to have colours, on as broad a palette as possible, not for the achievement of variety for its own sake but to create atmosphere and evoke moods (often long before the singer's entry), with an imaginative response to the words and the music, and also to the colours of different voices singing the same songs. There are wise words in this book about how to produce these sounds and colours, which of course apply to anyone wanting to play the piano well – arm weight, forget percussion, touch sensation, a portion of the brain in each finger tip, listen to yourself, squeeze a little harder with whatever finger is playing the main voice. To these essential pieces of advice I would only add (or expand) that the business of playing the piano should be one that is a total physical and human experience. Not just fingers and wrists striking keys on the keyboard, but stroking sounds out of the strings with physical activity which originates in the back, then energises shoulders, arms, wrists and all the links in between, and finally reaches, with a sense of total bodily involvement, the finger tips, which activate the keys to produce the sound one's mind and heart have heard just before the action of the piano carries this energy to the strings. How often does one hear playing, also from accompanists, where the only energy taking place is finger hitting key, and the brain isn't even in gear!

Having achieved a beautiful and/or appropriate tone, one has then to follow it with another and another and so begins phrasing. How fortunate we are to have the human voice to listen to, and to emulate, with our phrases. Here the ideal of human expression lies, coming, as it does, out of the human body, and being therefore a natural expression. Most of us instrumentalists have to work like the devil to attain phrasing that sounds natural and spontaneous, but how much more a singer has going for him when he has only(!) his body to use, creating his phrasing with breath, the original fact of life. We accompanists are often congratulated on the way we breathe with the singer; we are happy to be told too that we breathe *like* a singer, not so much as regards length of phrase, for we have no physical limitations on that score, but rather how the music is also supported and made flexible by the flow of our breathed phrases. All pianists are asked at some stage of their careers to play with a singing tone, which is often taken to mean only a metallic (precious or otherwise!) glint from the right hand's little finger; how much more important it is for all pianists, but especially accompanists whose permanent goal is to match and equal the human voice in beauty, flexibility, subtlety, and shape and expanse of phrasing, to be asked to play with our breath and thus make music in the same way as our singers, to the constant enhancement of all we do. Phrases can then follow to complement or contrast with each other, and so they are built into a musical edifice of satisfying shape, be it a song of one minute's duration, or "An die ferne Geliebte", or the Kreutzer Sonata.

Associated with this concept of phrases being breathed is the equally important one of rhythm – the pulse of music, not only in the sense of rhythms (like Polonaise, Waltz, March) but the very heart beat which is the other source of life to music.

All these things and many others are dealt with in *The Unashamed Accompanist*. I find in it once again a very succinct exposition of *all* the things I believe make a good accompanist. The advice is timeless, and all of it is invaluable. Gerald Moore tells us how to rehearse, how to play *legato*, with *rubato*, how to behave in the artists' room, how to make all one has rehearsed "come off", how to play orchestral accompaniments, folk songs, sonatas with various instruments, and one of the most vexed subjects of all, how to balance! That this is an accompanist's permanent concern is apparent from the fact that Gerald Moore's universally best-selling autobiography is called *Am I Too Loud?* One will never satisfy everyone in the solution of this problem, but the ideal, indeed the only satisfactory resolution lies in experience, the experience of the accompanist's ears, which can be acquired quite quickly, but always depending on the sensitivity with which he hears *himself*, as well as the singer – after all he is paid to do the latter!

I played a recital at the Royal Festival Hall in London in 1967 with Nathan Milstein. At the end I believed, and was told, it had gone well, but my belief was a bit shattered when I was handed by the impresario a folded page torn from the programme, out of which fell a pound note, whose presence was explained by the

Geoffrey Parsons.

words scribbled round the page's margin: "Use this for lessons from Gerald Moore on how not to play too loud." *Any* instruction from the Master should have cost a great deal Moore.

I was amused at the time some thirty years ago, and in retrospect, at a comment from Gerald Moore after I had very modestly and in great awe gone to the artists' room after a wonderful recital of his – there was a good singer too. I said I had particularly liked the Schumann. He said: "What was wrong with the rest of it?" Reassuring to know that the great, too, need reassurance, and a warning to all who would approach an artist at the peak of his or her sensibility after a good concert! Real artists are not afraid of constructive criticism from informed and respected sources, but I think all agree that the artists' room is not the place to hear it – even implied by absence of praise. Those who venture into the private domain of an artist after a performance which has included public expression of personal artistic ideals should not, at that moment, be critical, nor yet fulsome, but respond with whole-hearted expression of enjoyment.

I like the passage in which Gerald Moore describes his way of "drawing" tone from the piano. I would like to add another way I believe in to consolidate a pianist's relationship with his strings via his keyboard. I try to continue the contact as long as possible by a feeling of sliding in along the key further towards the source of the sound in the search for the ultimate tonal embrace. I am well aware that any physical motion after the key is depressed has no influence on the sound just played, but it helps to transfer the arm weight to the next note or chord, and the psychology suits me.

In his book Gerald Moore gives us, though as a comparatively young man, his views on how he achieved all that anyone with half an ear can hear in his recordings – his deep love and respect for his composers, particularly his beloved Schubert, and the intellect, heart, soul, and vivid imagination with which he brings their music to life – unashamed.

I doubt that he would want to change more than a few words these forty years on. In this time much has changed, however, in many of the circumstances in which an accompanist finds himself, and it is this very book which is responsible for beginning many of these improvements. We have all, performers and listeners alike, benefited from the advice in this book, and from Gerald's practice of his precepts in his playing in thousands of concerts and records.

Every accompanist has his own idea about how best to practise his profession, but I venture to suggest that I am not alone in finding the means of doing so remarkably similar to those recommended in this book. We may all be happy if our means produce results like Gerald Moore's – to say nothing of that instantly recognisable golden glowing sound.

With music and words he has made the world far more aware of his, and our, role. In gratitude and homage to him no accompanist can ever be too loud.

GEOFFREY PARSONS

The Unashamed Accompanist

The hands of Gerald Moore.

Introduction to this edition

THE FIRST EDITION of this little book, my initial attempt at authorship, saw the light during the 1939–45 War and due to the exigencies of that time, had to be condensed and finally issued as economically as possible. Walter Eastman of Messrs. Ascherberg, Hopwood and Crew, a firm of music publishers, came to me with the idea. *The Unashamed Accompanist* caught the imagination of a wide public. After a lapse of some twenty years, its impact having subsided, Messrs. Methuen and Company decided to revive it in a slightly larger edition which was received by the public and critics with indulgence: in due time this also faded away. I never expected to see a resurrection and felt that like darling Clementine it was lost and gone forever.

To my astonishment *The Unashamed* has come up for the third time, refloated by Julia MacRae Books. Julia MacRae wisely provided a pair of potent water wings to help it surface in the persons of two superb artists, Geoffrey Parsons, the accompanist of the day, and Graham Johnson, the accompanist of the morrow. I am more grateful than I can say for their generosity and brotherly (perhaps I ought to say filial) spirit.

This book was labelled "Unashamed" because that, in fact, describes my attitude. I never regarded myself as an accompanist *pro tem*, did not consider as so many have done, the playing of accompaniments as a stepping stone to worthier heights: the

[21]

accompanist's work is virtuous in itself. I wrote not only in the desire to indicate the lines along which a would-be follower of the gentle art of ensemble should work but with the ambition to arouse more interest in – and make clear the importance of – the accompaniment so that appreciation, enjoyment and the significant part it played could enrich those who did not know what they were missing.

But my chief object was to induce more piano students or amateur pianists to take up accompanying for their careers or for their pleasure. (The inexperienced cannot be expected to imagine the delight that ensemble work affords.) I recognize now that Sir Landon Ronald was not exaggerating when he declared that there was an abundance of virtuoso pianists in the world but precious few accompanists of the highest class.

For the more of us there are, the better: fiercer competition will breed a superior standard, this in its turn will affect and improve the work of the instrumentalist and singer who depend on the accompanist always for support, often for inspiration.

"Good accompanists are born but not made" is an axiom with which I profoundly disagree. Accompanying is an acquired art. A student can be guided a long way up the road that leads to proficiency, beyond that point, however, each individual has to learn and profit by searching self-criticism. That is to say a good teacher can teach a student to *play* the notes of an accompaniment quite beautifully for a start, but he cannot assess or adjust tonal balance where there is constant give and take between two partners, he cannot teach anticipation nor can he reliably indicate where it is desirable to retreat or to lead. So much, so very much, comes from the heart and the mind of the player himself. The true art of partnership will gradually dawn on the increasingly captivated player from the outcome of his own practical experience, patience, and perseverance, the blossoming of his own acute sensitivity and – most of all – his love.

This, so far as I am aware, was the first book to be devoted wholly to the work of the accompanist: therefore I was compelled for the furtherance of my argument to push the soloists upstage and focus the limelight on their partner. This *modus operandi* was excusable and inevitable in order to illustrate the importance of the role the accompanist plays.

On the concert platform the man at the piano seldom gets the limelight, and in truth he seldom deserves it. Again and again it is the singer who gives his very all, who lives and believes in his song, who pours out his heart and is finally depleted. Has the accompanist given his all? Has he matched or even approached the singer's generosity of feeling? Has he spent on his work the time, the pains, the devotion that it deserves?

Broadly, the answers to these questions when I wrote the above paragraph over forty years ago were decidedly in the negative.

The same reproach does not apply to-day, for the level the pianist-partner has reached is appreciably higher. Several causes, in my opinion, have contributed to this change.

First and foremost has been the example of our present day accompanists – Parsons, Johnson, Vignoles, Isepp, Willison, and at least a dozen more ensemble players who have brought to their work a penetration and mastery which has compelled attention, not on themselves as individuals, but on the music they were performing. They enhance the art of their partners.

Another factor in this development is the interest conductors and virtuoso pianists have shown in the ensemble sphere. When such men as Bruno Walter, Barenboim, Ashkenazy, Previn, Lupu, discovered what joy accompanying gave them and appeared on the concert platform in support of singers, the superficial (Philistine) listener must have had a dim inkling that there might be more in these piano parts than he had imagined: perhaps because of the prestige of these artists he was aware for the first time that there was such a thing as partnership.

And lastly, the music critic has played his part. Nowadays his review of recitals generally embraces the partner at the piano. It was not ever thus. The critics are coming on!

My modesty, though not excessive to the point of unhealthiness, impels me to apologize for my all too frequent use of the first person singular, but I could use no other formula when setting down these few thoughts.

GERALD MOORE

[23]

ONE

Partnership

WHY more students of the piano do not devote themselves to the art of accompaniment is a question that puzzles me. Possibly the answer is that there is more glory and glamour in the career of a solo pianist; his name is printed in big letters, whereas the accompanist's name is put at the foot of the bill – indeed, printers take a fiendish delight in using the smallest type available for it. A few students take up accompanying as an afterthought, because they have dropped by the wayside; the going has been too hard for them in the solo pianist's race, so they enter, grudgingly, the odd-looking ranks of accompanists. Such people achieve little success, however, as they are handicapped by two disadvantages – first, their training, apart from the technique of piano playing, does not give them the necessary equipment that an ensemble pianist needs; and secondly, their heart is not in the job, for they have one eye constantly cocked on the "senior" class of soloists, hoping to jump back there at the earliest opportunity.

Sir Landon Ronald said to me when I was a young man: "The world is over-stocked with brilliant solo pianists, but there are precious few good accompanists in the field." I thought at that time that accompanying was *infra dig*; I imagined the accompanist was a sort of caddie who carried the violinist's fiddle. But the advice of a fine musician such as Ronald was not to be disregarded, and after some years of work and experience I began to realize how important and interesting the musical life of an accompanist could and should be. The popular conception of an adequate accompanist (that is, of a quiet, modest individual of undoubted sobriety, neat

[25]

but not gaudy, seen but not heard, an affable automaton, obediently following the soloist and oozing with sympathy and discretion from every pore) was one that could not be reconciled
with the nature of the work I had to do. Only on the rarest occasion, I found, should the accompanist be satisfied with providing
an unobtrusive murmur in the background. Such an attitude
would ruin the works of composers of the first rank. The truth of
this is clear in the piano part to the violin piece "La fontaine
d'Aréthuse", by Szymanowski, or to the song "Der Erlkönig",
by Schubert and hundreds of other works I could mention.

The vital importance of the accompaniments in these difficult
examples is obvious, but they are not important merely because
of their technical difficulty. The piano part of the simplest song of
Schubert is just as important as that of the "Erl King", and because
of its simplicity, because of its bareness, gives the pianist who makes
any pretence of being musical much more to think about.

The partnership between singer and pianist is a fifty-fifty affair
as surely as it is between violinist and pianist, in, say, the Kreutzer
Sonata of Beethoven. That the fiddler may receive a bigger fee
than the piano accompanist (as distinct from the piano virtuoso),
that the singer's name may loom larger than his, that it is the big
name which draws at the box office, have nothing to do with it.
We must have souls above such mundane and sordid things.

The first question a violinist or a singer asks when he is offered
an engagement is "Who is the accompanist?" (If he is of a mercenary disposition he may first inquire about his fee, but the experience and ability of the accompanist will be his second and
most pressing question.) To the soloist, a good accompanist means
enjoyable work: enjoyable work means good work. It is a pity
some concert promoters do not attach as much importance to the
accompanist as does the soloist; the view that he contributes no
more to the success of the concert than the cloakroom attendant at
the other end of the hall is far too prevalent. The result is that the
average fee for the young accompanist, who has yet to make his
name, is not a high one. If the emoluments were made a little more
attractive there would be more inducement for serious students of
the piano to take up an accompanist's career. It follows that the

With the young Dietrich Fischer-Dieskau

all-round standard of performance would reach a higher level, for the man 'at the piano' can help to make or mar a concert.

No good composer writes an accompaniment as an after-thought, for it must be the basis of the whole musical structure. Any piece of music with a poorly written or poorly played accompaniment is a failure. It you want a picture of a dull, unimaginative accompaniment look at any of the Spanish dances of Sarasate. True, the fiddle writing is most grateful, for Sarasate was a great

[27]

violinist, but he knew next to nothing about the piano. In fact, Sarasate's accompaniments seem to have been an afterthought: they merely furnish a drab background. Consequently these pieces, while being "effective" in the cheap sense of the term, are valueless from a musical standpoint, chiefly because of the weakness of the pianoforte part.

No, the accompanist's opportunity will present itself in really fine music, and he must see to it that there is a proper partnership between the two parts, not because he, the man at the piano, wants to attract undue attention to himself, but because he owes it to the violinist or singer for whom he is playing, and above all he owes it to the composer. The pianist himself has everything to gain from this sharing of responsibility, for it will make his own work far more interesting, and, in addition, it will lighten the burden of the sensitive soloist. Of course the insensitive soloist will not notice it, and with him all the accompanist stands to lose is a little perspiration.

The work of the accompanist is one of the most varied in all music. In order to show the extent of his repertoire, here is a rough summary of it: the solo literature of the violin and the 'cello as well as the sonatas and concertos for these instruments; the pianoforte trios, &c.; the repertoire of opera and oratorio arias (operatic duets, quartets, &c.) and the enormous repertoire of songs (soprano, contralto, tenor, baritone, and bass) which may be in any language; accompaniments to solos for wind instruments – the oboe, flute, and clarinet. Have I left anything out? Possibly, but the list is endless.

Consider the variety in the style of playing and in the mental approach that is needed, for example, in the music of Schubert, on the one hand, and the music of Debussy, on the other. The styles of these two composers are poles apart, just as the German language is from the French, as the poetry of Goethe is from the poetry of Verlaine. And we accompanists must be expert in and intimate with each. Soloists have this advantage over us: that the violinist is not obliged to learn the music written for the 'cello; sopranos are not, so far as I am aware, obliged to learn bass songs. Again, soloists may specialize. A singer may specialize in French songs, or in German songs; violinists may specialize in Bach. But not accompanists: we must be all things to all men. On successive days we may be called on to play a recital of Spanish songs, then the two Brahms clarinet or viola sonatas and then the song cycle "Die Winterreise" (Winter's Journey) of Schubert, a recital of modern French songs (or, shall we say, Russian, Scandinavian, or Italian songs) and we may round off a not exceptional week with a violinist whose speciality is Mozart and Beethoven. Such a list of engagements would not worry an accompanist if he were an experienced artist, although I cannot deny I have known occasions when I have sunk into the depths of an arm-chair in the Artists' Room with a sigh of relief, while the fiddler or 'cellist played an unaccompanied Bach suite – beyond my hearing, of course. At the risk of being accused of musical pedantry or snobbishness, I declare I am all in favour of unaccompanied Bach; in fact, I am the most sympathetic accompanist in the world, when it comes to anything unaccompanied.

I repeat my question: Why do not more piano students divert their attention from solo work and devote themselves to accompanying? There is plenty of work for all of us; the more there are, the keener the competition will be, and in consequence our work will attain a higher standard. Then, and only then, will the status of the accompanist be raised, and we shall be recognized as artists in our own right, and not mere accessories.

My advice to anyone desirous of becoming an accompanist is simple and can be easily followed. Tell a teacher of singing that you are a pianist and that you place yourself at his or her disposal to play for singing lessons. This may be humdrum at first, but here you will take the first step towards learning how to accompany, you will learn singers' ways and a little about voice production; you will begin to lay a foundation for the enormous repertoire that the fully fledged accompanist needs. After some months of this, the teacher will ask you to coach one or two of the pupils on your own (keeping them in time, correcting their wrong notes, &c.), and later more people will come to you for this type of work. The result of all this is that you are now a professional accompanist, poor but honest. You will eventually get plenty of work in the studio and in public if you take your work seriously and regard your job as a full time one.

In England today there are many good women accompanists who play for music teachers' classes, or who are used for "coaching" purposes. But they never seem to get known, or to emerge from the studio; this is because of an oldfashioned prejudice held by many soloists who say: "I do like to have a man at the piano." At the risk of queering my own pitch, I ask why must it be a man? In these days when women can turn their hand to anything, this seems a bigoted outlook to me. Personally, if I were a soloist I should raise no objection to a lady accompanying me – anywhere.

I do not feel ashamed to call myself an accompanist, and yet to many that title is a brand signifying that the owner is of a slightly inferior caste. My loving aunt is not the only one who asks me why I do not become a solo pianist – even musicians have asked me the same question. Yet somebody must play accompaniments, and that is the work that I love. If men such as Nikisch, Bruno Walter, Hamilton Harty, Barenboim, Ashkenazy and Previn could do it, then it is good enough for me – and you.

Some tennis players and golfers prefer singles to the partnership game, but I like partnership. So let the solo pianist have the thrill and the glory of playing a lone hand, I shall continue, I hope, to get my musical thrill from collaboration and from the joy that comes from perfect team work.

TWO

Preparation

I LAY so much stress on the importance of the accompanist study-ing a song before he rehearses it with a singer, that I want to urge the beginner not to hesitate to communicate with the singer he is going to accompany, to get his music, and master it in detail.

All accompanists ought to have a library of their own, consisting of all the songs of Schubert, Wolf, Schumann, Brahms, Debussy, Fauré, &c.; and a representative selection of old and modern English songs. The expense in these days of accumulating such a collection is obvious, but the student, if he cannot get in touch with his singer, can borrow from his musical friends or from a lending library.

A singer is delighted if he is told that his accompanist knows the songs before the rehearsal commences.

Artists coming to my studio from abroad with obscure songs of whose existence I was supposed to be ignorant have said to me, "Here are some new songs. At least, they will be new to you."

"Not at all, I know them intimately." (Sensation!)

Of course I did not tell these dear people that I had been prac-tising these very songs until the moment of their arrival.

THE FIRST thing an accompanist should study when he has to play a new song is the words. It is stupid to pretend to play a song with any understanding if he does not know what it is all about. This seems an obvious statement, but unfortunately it is necessary to make it. I have heard accompanists, amateur and professional, playing songs in their own mother tongue as if the words were no concern of theirs whatever. The accompaniment to every good song paints a picture or evokes a mood which is inspired by the words. The composer did not write the vocal line first and then fill in the piano part afterwards; they were both born in his brain at the same time. Therefore the accompanist and the singer, the one no less than the other, owe all to the words and depend on the words to guide them.

How extremely awkward for the accompanist when he has to play German, French, Russian, Italian, and Scandinavian songs if he knows nothing of these languages. I am not trying to frighten the would-be accompanist by suggesting he should be a master of six languages, but I do suggest that a working knowledge of French and German will save him much searching in a dictionary. Many of the well-known songs of Schubert, Wolf, Schumann, Brahms, Debussy, Fauré, &c., have English translations, which will give the beginner a good outline of the meaning of the original poem. Sometimes, however, these translations are so unpoetic and inaccurate that a more ambitious student will be anxious to consult his dictionary occasionally to find out the literal meaning of some of the words. There is no excuse for the accompanist not knowing the literal meaning of every word of a German song, or even a French song for that matter. (I am inclined to lay more emphasis on the German Lied, since the greatest song writers of the world were, in my opinion, Schubert and Wolf.) What is the poor pianist to do, you may ask, when playing songs by Granados the Spaniard, or Grieg the Norwegian, Moussorgsky the Russian, or Malipiero the Italian? Well, let him ask the singer to give him the literal meaning of each line or at the very least the gist of the poem, sufficient, in fact, to give him a picture to work on, so that he knows what colour the background requires, and is aware of the salient features in the foreground that must be made to glow. Failure on the part of the accompanist to understand the poem, to appreciate the significance of the words, will ruin any decent song, and the accompaniment will sound meaningless and dead.

I remember playing once for a Chinese singer, and sad to tell, my knowledge of the Chinese language is more than somewhat restricted. The singer, however, came to my rescue and explained as best he could the meaning of the words. Without doubt, the inkling I had from him made my playing more sympathetic, if I may use that humdrum word in this particular sense, and helped me to contribute a little more to the partnership.

What character can an accompanist give to his playing of strophic songs if he is ignorant of the words? It is not only folk songs which are written in this style; Schubert and Brahms, to name two composers only, have set poems of three, four, or more verses where each verse is musically – note for note – the same. It is pitiful to see, or hear, a singer trying to fire his singing with imagination and life, trying to vary his tone according to the mood of the poem, while the accompanist sits at the piano like a tired old horse, blissfully ignorant of anything that is going on. He is an impediment to his partner. The intelligent singer takes the words for guidance, and according to their meaning will make one verse different from another by some slight rhythmical fluctuation, by variations in phrasing, breathing, and dynamics. How stimulating for him to feel his pianist responding eagerly to the poem's changing pictures and moods.

No accompanist in his senses would play all the verses of the folk song "O, no John", or the different verses of Brahms's "Vergebliches Ständchen" (Vain Suit) in exactly the same way. Yet, in these transparent examples no great credit should be claimed by the accompanist who succeeds in characterizing them, for all he has to do, broadly speaking, is to differentiate between gaiety and dolefulness, between the girl's voice and the boy's. Much more subtlety of expression is needed in strophic songs of a less frivolous nature, such as Schubert's "Das Wandern" (Wandering), which has five verses, "Die liebe Farbe" (The Favourite Colour), which has three verses, "Des Baches Wiegenlied" (The Brook's Lullaby), five verses.

Let me repeat, the key to the situation is the words. I shall try to explain in the next chapter how the pianist can attempt to vary his playing according to the story the singer is relating.

Nothing but the words will keep the accompanist from going completely off the track in a song where the composer, I say it with all deference, has missed the mark. "Waft ye gentle breezes" is the

[33]

A master-class with Gerald Moore.

first line in Brahms's song "Botschaft" (The Message), yet the accompaniment, in spite of the instruction *piano*, looks like a cavalry charge and can sound like one unless played with the greatest thought and care.

Possibly Brahms when he wrote this was picturing a galloping horse and the sounding of the Post-horn (as Schubert did in his song "The Post"), but there is no allusion to all this in the words "Waft ye gentle breezes to the cheek of my beloved". Composers do miss it sometimes, and it requires all the accompanist's ingenuity and technique to make a piano part sound convincing and apt.

Most unfortunate results will attend the accompanist who does not know what he is playing about – what the singer is singing about. A young friend of mine was playing the accompaniment to me one day of Wolf's song "Bitt' ihn, O Mutter" (Beg Him, O Mother). This accompaniment is written with Wolf's usual eloquence and urgency, but it was played by this young lady with such viciousness that I ventured to ask her if she knew what "Bitt' ihn, O Mutter" meant. "Of course," she replied. "It means 'O Mother, bite him.' "

THREE

Practising

TONE QUALITY. – There are two things of the most vital importance that a pianist has to learn whether he wishes to be a solo pianist or an accompanist. The first thing is to learn to listen to himself, and the second is the same. I think that this is the most difficult thing for a pianist to learn. The singer has to create his note and cultivate the quality of it – so does the string player. They are rightly taught that their paramount aim is to produce a beautiful quality of tone. They have the process of searching for their notes, then producing them, and finally cultivating them. It is a natural process for them to listen with the greatest intentness, because, allied to their admirable fetish for a beautiful quality of tone, is their anxiety about their intonation.

They know that nobody can listen with pleasure to them if they sing or play out of tune. This, I believe, explains why, generally speaking, they listen to themselves much more carefully than many pianists seem to do. A violinist knows that unless he exercises constant care his violin can produce an ugly tone, even though it be a magnificent Stradivarius.

We pianists are not always so careful: we see the notes grinning in front of us and we just slap them down; we have no worry about intonation, nobody can accuse us of playing out of tune, and so we leave it at that – forgetting what the violinist could tell us, that our fine instrument can still be made to sound ugly.

We can make the excuse that the fiddler's tone comes from under his ear while our keyboard is in the region of our waist and our tone rises a couple of feet away from us: much more difficult –

much less intimate – but all the more reason for us to be wary, to exercise the most constant care.

To make his tone blend with a singer or a violinist it is incumbent on the accompanist to cultivate the quality of his tone. Can this be done? Yes, by listening intelligently so that his ears can detect instantly the difference between good and bad tone and by learning to use his fingers with sensitiveness and variety of touch. If the fingers respond obediently to the brain they will satisfy the ear.

Imagine that a portion of your brain is in each finger-tip, and eventually you will get a touch sensation according to the variety of tone you want to produce. Test yourself first of all by striking the chord of C major. Strike it with strength, with your hands shaped like a talon and your wrist stiff, the result will be a hard, metallic tone. Now strike the same chord with your fingers shaped in the same way but your wrist loose (not letting the arch of your knuckles collapse but allowing your wrist to "give" on impact) and you will get a firm, strong tone but without the hardness that the first chord had.

If you can detect no difference, it is the fault of your ears and you must continue experimenting with this exercise until your ears tell you that they are aware. Try the same experiment with single notes. Dig into the note stiff-jointedly with the very tip of your finger to obtain the hard tone. Then try depressing the note, but still with the weight of your forearm behind it and contacting the note (not this time with the very tip of the finger – but with the finger less aggressively curled) nearer the ball of the finger. This time a warm, singing tone should be the result.

Your "touch sensation" must habituate itself to this singing tone. Practise it on all your fingers and in the five-finger exercise – not only in C major but chromatically through all the keys. Do not stop at single notes while using this touch. Get a hymn tune and play an octave bass with your left hand and take the soprano, alto, and tenor voices with your right. Now try to make the soprano sing clearly over the other voices. In order to get the extra amount of tone from the soprano voice you will have to squeeze a little harder with whatever finger is playing the soprano voice.

You will have to resist the impact more with this finger; to do this – in other words – this finger will have to be a little less yielding on contact with the keys than the other fingers. Do not be satisfied until you can give this same treatment to the alto voice – and then the tenor voice. Listen most carefully as you do it, and guard against the tendency – in your anxiety to make the note predominate – of sounding the singing note a fraction earlier than the other notes in the chord.

All the notes must be sounded simultaneously.

The first page of Schubert's "Im Frühling" (In Springtime) from which the above example is taken is a good song to practise in this way, making the soprano voice in the piano part sing. The opportunity to do this will come often. We find it in the three-part harmony of the right hand in Schubert's "An die Musik" (To Music). We have two golden opportunities to sing here when after each verse the pianist takes up the song from the singer. And we should make it our aim to sing as sweetly as he.

Many such songs come to my mind – where by the employment of a singing touch we may carry on where the singer – as if his heart were too full – leaves it to us. Schumann's "Du bist wie eine Blume" (Thou art lovely as a flower) for instance is another example, the postlude of which should be played with a golden tone, singing, squeezing the juice out of each note of the melody –

playing even the grace notes before the final chord with a slow dwelling on each note as if with reluctance to bring the song to an end.

The soprano voice in the accompaniment often has to sing but naturally there are occasions when the bass notes have the solo, the opening bars of "To Music" and "Who is Sylvia?" for example. Here your right hand accompanies your left hand and in "To Music" should be kept close to the keyboard all the time; the chords must be played in parenthesis and with great smoothness.

Forget percussion: coax the sound out of the piano, and to join one chord to the next, use your sustaining pedal lightly, but frequently. Sometimes the inner voice must be raised above the others as in the middle section of Vaughan Williams' "Silent Noon".

Very often the most vital note in a chord (vital because it shows an impending or accomplished change of key) will come in one of these inner voices and it is then, as I have said before, that the finger which has to make this note prominent must meet the pianoforte key with more resistance than the other fingers.

You must not feel, once you have learned to produce a good singing tone, that the training of the ear and the touch are completed.

It is by experimenting with touch that the accompanist will learn to produce a variety of tone colours. He can produce a sharp tone whilst still obeying the composer's instructions to play *piano*. He can get a fat round tone without being metallic. Weight can be produced without noise. The softest tones can be produced to carry. The meaning of the poem and his future collaboration with the singer will help him to know what touch to use and when to employ it.

Armed indeed with a knowledge of the words and with so many varieties of touch at his command, the pianist will find the dullest looking pianoforte parts interesting. He will be able to colour his playing according to the words. "Das Wandern" (Wandering) and such strophic songs as those with which Schubert's cycle "Die schöne Müllerin" (The Miller's Daughter) abounds will become thrilling experiences for the accompanist, and consequently will be more alive to the singer and the audience. For instance, when the singer refers in the second verse of "Wandering" to the running stream, the accompanist should try to make the semi-quaver figure in the right hand ripple and run.

The third verse refers to the millwheel, and the same figure should now be used with a weightier and less *legato* touch, as he sees in his mind's eye the splashing waters and the millwheel turning.

The heavy mill stones are pictured in the next verse, and here he plays ponderously with his left hand.

LEGATO PLAYING. – I have not mentioned *legato* playing yet, but this obviously must come under the general heading of touch. Important – even vital – though the use of the sustaining pedal may be to us, we must not rely on it altogether for smooth sustained playing. In accompaniments of block harmony the pedal may see us through – but it is simply not good enough to jam the pedal down and hope for the best in songs with *arpeggiando* accompaniments where the harmony is constantly changing.

The sustaining pedal must, of course, be used in these *arpeggiando* accompaniments and also whenever we want a singing tone, but the use of the sustaining pedal is so abused by many amateurs that perhaps I may be forgiven if at this point I suggest a good exercise for pedalling. Go back to your five-finger exercise or your scale, but this time play it extremely slowly: raise your hands clear of the keyboard after each note, but before quitting the key with your finger catch the tone with your sustaining pedal and release it as you strike the next note. There must be no gap in the tone.

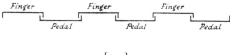

Practise this at an ever-increasing speed until you can pedal so deftly that there is never any fear of blurring between one note and the next.

It is not always necessary or possible to give a separate pedal to each note in rapid passages; here the pedal is changed with the harmony.

In these *arpeggiando* songs I would give one general word of advice and that is, forget bar lines. I have heard what might have been good *legato* playing quite spoilt by the slavish accentuation of the first beat of the bar, or any other so-called strong beats which may occur. Just because the piece of music is written in $\frac{4}{4}$ time, the composer does not always want the first and third beats emphasized. As an experiment play Schumann's "In der Fremde" (In a Strange Land) and the first section of Brahms's "O wüsst" ich doch den Weg zurück" (O, Could I Return) with accents on the first beat of each bar, and then afterwards play them with no accents whatever, and the difference will be obvious. The first way will be heavy and square, but the other will float and have gentle curves.

Legato playing and evenness of touch are problems in such songs as Schubert's "Wohin?" (Whither?) and Mendelssohn's "Auf Flügeln des Gesanges" (On Wings of Song). I said earlier that the accompanist must not be satisfied merely to provide an unobtrusive murmur in the background. Here I contradict myself, for in these two songs it is precisely what he has to do.

To make these *arpeggiando* accompaniments a quiet murmur, it is necessary to take some care. In the Schubert song your fingers should be on the keys all the time, even after the notes have been released. Each finger is then ready and in position to depress the key when required to do so, and does not have to make a leap to keep its next appointment.

TONE QUANTITY. – A trap into which any musician can fall is the misjudging of his own quantity of tone. This is what I mean. A *piano* is marked on the music and from it a long and gradual *crescendo* is marked leading to a *forte*, not content with that, the composer asks for another *crescendo* leading to a *fortissimo*.

The poor player finds too late that his first *crescendo* was too steep, his *forte* is too big – it is a *fortissimo*. Consequently, he is incapable of meeting the further demands for more tone that the composer makes on him. Conversely, making a *diminuendo* from a *forte* to a *piano* and thence to a *pianissimo*, he may find that he is already playing as softly as it is possible for him to play at the *piano* sign and he has no room left to get softer. A mistake like this has the same common denominator as has poor tone quality – it is failure to listen properly and concentratedly.

We should all have a standard of tone values. We should be keenly aware of the difference between a *pianissimo* and a *piano*, between a *piano* and a *mezzo piano*, a *mezzo piano* and a *mezzo forte*, &c., and as we practise we should make sure we observe this standard of values. This is most important, but we must not be hidebound over it. We cannot adhere to the same standard in every piece of music. The *piano* mark in Brahms's "Von ewige Liebe" (Eternal Love) is of a darker, fuller flavour than the *piano* in the same composer's "Wiegenlied" (Lullaby). Similarly, the *forte* in "Nachtigall" (Nightingale) by Brahms is lighter and more singing than the heavy ponderous *forte* in "Der Schmied" (The Smith).

But this is not to say that Brahms is to blame. It only goes to show that there are more varieties of tone and colour than there are labels such as *piano* or *pianissimo* to tag on to them. The composer (as we have seen in the strophic song) pays us the compliment of crediting us with a little imagination. This we can use when we have a knowledge of the words, plus the composer's markings, plus our intelligent ears. Our standard of tone values therefore must be elastic and vary according to the type of music we are playing. This standard of values varies, of necessity, with each singer with whom we collaborate.

COMPOSER'S MARKINGS. – I am a great believer, in spite of what I may have said about the pianist using his imagination, in trying to obey implicitly the instructions on the music, especially if the work I am studying is by a great composer. I do not think, for instance, that we should make a *crescendo* or a *diminuendo* unless the composer asks for it, and the same applies to a *rallentando* or *accelerando*. Indeed, by obeying the composer we shall avoid several slovenly and amateurish habits. I am thinking of that tiresome

Gerald Moore gives a lecture recital.

trick of making a *rallentando* in the pianoforte introduction or interlude in a song prior to the entry of the voice, as if we knew in advance that the singer would not "come in" unless we "nursed" him in. This attitude of mind assumes that the singer is of a low musical intelligence. But at this juncture – not having yet rehearsed with him – we might give him the benefit of the doubt, always remembering that most singers nowadays are good musicians. We might take the trouble, too, of looking at a few of Schubert's songs, picked at random, and see how rarely the composer asks for a *molto rallentando* at the close of his songs. We all commit this sin occasionally, perhaps thinking we know better than Schubert; or making the excuse – if we are aware we are making a great *allargando* – that Schubert forgot to put it in.

How much easier it is for us, too, to neglect the rests that the composer has gone to the trouble to put in his score. We frequently go to sleep in the rests by treading on the sustaining pedal with our heavy foot, whereas the object of the composer in using the "rest" sign is often to galvanize us into liveliness. Schubert has written 153 rests in 48 bars of music in "Heidenröslein" (The Hedgerose), and if we ignore them the song is robbed of its freshness. The same applies to Schubert's "Geheimes" (Secret), where the proper observance of the rests – under the singer's *legato* line – gives us the sparkle and playfulness which are the song's essence.

We are apt to be almost as slovenly over accents. In "Gefrorne Tränen" (Frozen Tears)

Schubert has set us a pretty problem by the false accenting of one hand against the other, and it is only by solving this, in observing all the accents, that we shall come nearer the effect that Schubert wanted.

Wrong notes may at times be forgiven, for we accompanists are only human, after all (though even this has been questioned), but it is inexcusable for us to neglect the composer's markings or to super-impose our own.

SIMPLE SONGS THAT NEED PRACTISING. – The reader may gather that it is not only technically difficult accompaniments which must be practised. The simpler the accompaniment, the more food for thought it will give to the sensitive pianist.

To take an example, there are many solo pianists who will give a first-rate performance of Liszt's E flat Concerto or Tschaikovsky's B flat minor Concerto, but it takes an artist to play Beethoven's Piano Concerto in G major. So it is with accompaniments. Passages and pieces of technical difficulty must, of course, be worked at, but many accompanists do not take enough time or trouble over slow, simple-looking tunes. I maintain that to play such a song as the "Erl King" does not require nearly so much thought or care as the playing of Schubert's "Litany" and "Du bist die Ruh'" (Thou Art Peace to Me). In these songs each note has to be played with due regard to the note that preceded it and to the note that succeeds it and be properly proportioned to the whole musical sentence. In the last-named song the pianoforte interlude, for example, has a "turn" which needs handling with deliberation.

Should this turn be executed with the slightest semblance of brilliance or slickness it will put an end to any thought of reverent contemplation. My suggested shaping of this phrase stretches or lengthens the third beat – but no matter.

[47]

These songs must be treated reverently; indeed, in such deeply serious or religious songs the usage of the golden singing tone we have been at such pains to cultivate should be eschewed. A *crescendo* or *diminuendo* mark should be obeyed with the tenderest solicitude, and not made the excuse for an exaggerated nuance.

These songs must be practised with concentration on tone and tone gradation and we must listen critically to the quality of tone we are producing and to the quantity of tone in relation to what has gone before, and what comes after. A song to practise along these lines is Wolf's "Auf ein altes Bild" (On gazing on an old picture). It is in four part harmony throughout. We should listen jealously as we pass from one chord to the next, and must not let it be smutched by any semblance of a broken or *arpeggiando* chord. Graceful passes in the air with our hands are not wanted here.

Do not be deceived, these songs are not so easy as they look. We are fine fellows no doubt, and can spank our way valiantly through the "Erl King", ripple deliciously through Strauss's "Serenade", but we should approach "Du bist die Ruh'", "Litany", and "Auf ein altes Bild" not only with respect but with humility.

RHYTHM. – Can the accompanist develop in himself a sound, safe sense of rhythm to which the singer can cling like a ship to an anchor? It is most necessary that he should do so; a song can be wrecked if the accompanist has weak and flabby rhythm.

If you do not believe me, wait for some suitable occasion when a tenor friend may be sustaining a top A in the middle of a phrase, or in the middle of a word. He has to stick on this A until you have played three bars before he can come down and finish his word, or phrase. Try a curious experiment by letting your accent lack bite or your tempo slacken, and, to use Osmin's words: "Where is your charming creature then?" Probably dying of asphyxiation and in the vilest temper.

Your rhythm must be sure and steady. Practise "Hark, hark, the Lark", "Ungeduld" (Impatience), and "Atlas" of Schubert; the "Second Venetian Song" and the "Two Grenadiers", by Schumann; "Der Gärtner" (The Gardener) and "Fussreise" (A Morning Walk), by Wolf. Here, indeed, you must have accent, the weight of which will depend on the character of the song. In

"Hark, hark, the Lark" and in "The Gardener" your accents must be light and bouncing. In "Atlas" they must be like thunderbolts, and at the end of the "Two Grenadiers" like the bass drum in a military band. Where rhythm is the backbone of a song, it is the accents which will hold you together and keep you steady. The metronome is a slight help, but you must learn to rely on yourself until the pulse of the song is part of you, until once the tempo being agreed on, you would not, could not, deviate one iota from the iron-bound rhythm which certain songs require.

DEXTERITY. – While I am aware that to many pianists the songs I have so far quoted make no demands on the player's dexterity (he who thinks that I am making mountains out of mole-hills will not be the man to play those songs as they should be played), this does not mean that I lightly pass over prodigiously difficult songs that would tax the powers of the greatest virtuosi. These gentry when they do condescend to play accompaniments, however, are often only interested in playing the "Erl King" of Schubert, "Der Feuerreiter" (The Fire Rider) of Wolf, and so on. Their performance of these works is not without grandeur and leaves us ordinary mortals gasping – it is only when we are slowly recovering from our daze that we recall that there was a singer too, but we failed to hear him.

Merely to play the notes of the "Erl King" is difficult – but it is much more difficult to play it as Schubert wanted it played. Most of the time the ruling sign which we must endeavour to obey is *piano*. Of course it is much easier to play *forte* but the great techni-cal difficulty here – aside from the playing of the notes – *is* to play *piano*.

Other types of songs there are, still of great difficulty though less tragic than the "Erl King", where our playing must sound carefree and easy. The difficult passages must be practised slowly, until we can play them without having to think about each individual note.

If we are worrying about notes there will be little joy in our playing. A friend once said to me after a performance: "I did not notice much gladness in your playing of Mozart's 'Allelujah'." Now in this song, which is not of great difficulty, there are one or two quick passages in thirds. Doubtless I was thinking about my

[49]

thirds. In other words my "fourth finger" stood in the way of my jubilation.

INDEPENDENCE OF EYE AND HAND. – It may now be thought that the accompanist is ready to rehearse with the singer. He has studied the words, he has mastered the difficult technical passages, he has satisfied himself that he is doing what the composer wants him to do. His playing is free from anxiety, but he is not (I am sorry to say, gentle reader,) quite ready to rehearse with the singer. He must learn now to forget his fingers, to let his eye dwell on the vocal line. He must – after carefully locking all the doors, if he has a voice like mine – hum and later sing the vocal line, uttering the same words that the singer will have to utter. This will correct any tendency he may have had to adopt a false tempo. He will see that a certain phrase must be sung in one breath, and he may have to quicken slightly the tempo of the whole song to make this possible. He will make a mental note of the place where he believes the singer will breathe – for singers have to breathe, regrettable though this may be, and arrange his playing and phrasing accordingly.

THESE ARE the lines along which the serious accompanist must work. These are the thoughts which should be nagging at his brain throughout his practising and worry him when he is away from the piano. By such practising the serious student will reap many benefits, his ears will become more highly sensitized, his touch more beautiful, his pedalling exact. By such thinking his playing will become altogether more sensitive.

I wish I could lay my hand on my heart and say I always worked in this way over every new song that I play. It would not be true. But this I can say, that my performance suffers when I have failed to do it.

"Please give me something more than the mere notes," a great singer once said to me as I played the introduction to a simple looking song. "Not just the notes."

I have always remembered that.

FOUR

Rehearsing

THE STUDIO of the accompanist is the meeting place between himself and the soloist. Sometimes it is the scene of battle, but luckily not often. He will welcome there soloists of all shapes and sizes, of all races and creeds, from the prima donna flowering in her fullest bloom, cleaving the air with the majesty of a ship in full sail, to the trembling debutante. There will come thin violinists, fat 'cellists, and the curiously pure-looking players of the flute. Tenors will come too and relate their recent successes. The wise accompanist will treat old or young, famous or unknown, with equal consideration.

"The first time I entered your studio to rehearse with you for my debut," a young singer once said to a well-known accompanist, "you made me feel I was an artist, and not a beginner."

If she had given him time to think of a reply, he might have answered: "Every serious student aspires to be an artist, every serious artist is a student."

Just because yesterday we were associated with a world famous star is no reason for giving ourselves airs before an inexperienced young soloist today.

The preliminary work the accompanist has done will enable him at the rehearsal to focus his attention and his ears on the singer. Rehearsal time will not be taken up by fumbling for the notes, worrying about pianoforte passages, by giving or exchanging involved explanations, but by getting down to the interpretation of the music. Many of the songs will have been in the singer's repertoire for years, and it will inspire him with confidence to hear the accompanist playing with authority at the first rehearsal. He will have no reason to exclaim, like a certain prima donna, "My patience is exhausted."

This may be the first time the accompanist has heard this singer; he may know nothing of his style, his tempo, or his conception of the song. Yet the accompanist's playing must not be tentative. If there is an introduction to the song he should deal with it in an authoritative manner, any differences between him and the singer over the tempo can be discussed later. He establishes a tempo which seems to him to be the right one, and then hopes for the best. At the entry of the voice the pianist must keep his eyes skinned, for the first two notes of the singer (unless they are sustained notes over a moving accompaniment) will give him the tempo that the singer finds most suitable. On hearing the first two notes of the voice in Schumann's "Two Grenadiers", for example, an accompanist can judge the singer's tempo for the whole song and adjust himself accordingly.

If, however, the singer has long sustained notes over a moving figure in the pianoforte part, as in Schubert's "Nacht und Träume" (Night and Dreams), he gets no such indication and should discuss it with the singer.

Indeed, the singer is helpless in such a case as this: what can he do if the accompanist adopts the wrong tempo? I remember hearing a most distinguished artist singing Schubert's "Ave Maria" and

Roles reversed: Gerald Moore sings, with Dame Janet Baker at the piano and record producer Ronald Kinloch Anderson looking on.

can still see the terror in her eyes as she heard her accompanist play the introductory bars so very slowly that she realized it would be impossible to sustain her vocal line without breathing in the middle of phrases or words.

BREATHING. – It is understood that the accompanist's eyes are riveted on the words and the vocal line, so that when the singer

[53]

phrases he phrases too, and when the singer breathes he is not caught unawares.

"It is wonderful to hear So-and-so playing for his wife. He breathes with her." What bosh! It does not need half as many breaths to play "Nacht und Träume" (Night and Dreams) as it takes to sing it, and what is more, he should try to cover up his wife's breaths as much as he possibly can, to fill up whatever holes her breathing has caused in the flow of the music and disguise them. He must not draw attention to them, for a breath may have to be taken in the middle of a phrase, and an allowance of time is necessary for this. In order that the gap in the singing should not be noticed, the accompanist must help her to glide over this hiatus by easing the tempo slightly before it and carrying on with the tempo smoothly afterwards. This is not so complicated as it seems, especially if the soloist is able to snatch a breath quickly and quietly. Not all the camouflage in the world can hide a singer's inhalation if it has the power and noise of a vacuum cleaner.

(Sometimes, of course, the accompanist should take his hands off the keyboard and release his sustaining pedal, taking off his tone at the same moment as the singer does, thus making a noticeable gap in the music. This should be a rehearsed effect and should be done either for dramatic emphasis or to precede and to ensure a perfectly timed attack from both of them on the next note.)

The accompanist must learn to judge the breath capacity of the singer. It is splendid if the latter can sing through the long phrases of Brahms's "Mainacht" (May Night), the same composer's "Feldeinsamkeit" (Alone in the Fields), or Vaughan Williams' "Silent Noon" without having to breathe in the middle of them. To help the singer achieve this the accompanist may be required to make a slight *accelerando* (so slight that it is imperceptible to the listener) as he nears the end of the phrase if he feels that the singer's breath is giving out. One hopes, however, not to have to do this – it is almost better if the singer takes a catch breath between two words. This is arranged at rehearsal.

PHRASING AND RUBATO. – I read in a newspaper not so very long ago that the accompanist "followed obediently". A good accompanist does not "follow", for following means "going after". "Follow that car!" shouts the detective to the taxi-driver, and that is precisely what the driver does in the novel, but precisely what the accompanist must not do. We rehearse in order that we shall not have to follow, that we shall be able to anticipate, and march abreast of the soloist. It often happens that the soloist justifiably alters the length of his stride or quickens his pace. Although every song has a basic tempo, you cannot perform many pieces of music through from beginning to end metronomically. A Chopin Nocturne played this way would be frightful. Composers use the equivalents of the comma, the full stop, and the paragraph; they use phrase marks as an indication for the punctuation they want. They expect a phrase to be elastic, not rigid; to be slightly quicker here, slightly slower there, but it will not be difficult for an accompanist to keep abreast of a singer who has a musical sense of *rubato*. There are singers whose *rubato* is so illogical and whose phrasing is so exaggerated that it is necessary for the pianist to go through the phrase several times before he and the singer are at one. Again, the singer, not being an automaton, may not necessarily sing a certain phrase twice in the same way. He may start it slowly and finish it quickly, or vice versa. If a phrase curves up and then down he may give the notes at the top of the curve more stress and more time, robbing the bottom notes of the curve to do this. The first and second lines of Vaughan Williams' "Silent Noon" have this curve. They read:

> *"Your hands lie open in the long fresh grass;*
> *The finger points look through like rosy blooms."*

Each of these lines has an ascending and then a descending curve. In the musical phrase the words "long" and "rosy" are the top of the arch, and the singer may dwell on these notes a fraction longer. In order to do this without disturbing the rhythm, he may rob the two earlier notes and the two following notes of some of their time value. This is not only legitimate, it is the proper way to phrase – always provided that it is not exaggerated beyond the bounds of good taste. (It has no relation whatever to the habit of the unmusical singer who, oblivious of the flight of time, will stick on a top note *ad infinitum*.)

All accompanists must be alive to these fluctuations. No helpful singer will object to going through a phrase many times with an accompanist who has difficulty in anticipating his intentions. Half the battle is for the accompanist to know the song, so that he can anticipate this *rubato*. Until he is absolutely certain he knows what the singer is going to do he will find his hands will respond to his brain a split second quicker if he keeps them down on the keyboard, with his fingers on the notes, and his eyes never off the vocal line. It cannot be too strongly emphasized that the accompanist's knowledge of the words is the key to the situation.

BALANCE. – The problems that have faced the accompanist so far should not be insurmountable and they are problems, moreover, on which he may seek advice, but these problems fade into insignificance beside the next one. This is balance. The accompanist alone is responsible for the balance between his instrument and the voice and nobody can help him. His dearest friend may rush into the artists' room after the first half of a recital and say that the piano cannot be heard, and at the same time the singer will be red in the face from exhaustion and rage because he thinks *he* cannot be heard. Half the audience will think the pianist was too timid, the other half that he was too bold. (It must be understood that the above remarks refer to concerts, and not to broadcasting and recording, where the balance is in the hands of a controller who can diminish or augment your tone by the turning of a little knob.)

This problem of balance is continually rearing its ugly head in my path, and it has to be solved afresh every time I perform. How does one solve it? You are never sure you have done so, but bitter experience will teach you a great deal. There are many things to be taken into account, such as the size and acoustics of the room or hall, the size and carrying power of the singer's voice, the tessitura of the song. At the rehearsal you adjust your volume according to the weight of the singer's voice as it sounds in your studio, always remembering that at the performance in a concert hall you will have to readjust yourself. The singer will throw his voice to the back of the hall, and you must do the same with your tone, so that not only the biggest *fortissimo* but the smallest *pianissimo* will travel clearly to the back row (not only because the music critics may be sitting and sleeping there, but because if your tone reaches there everybody in the hall will have heard it).

Has it ever occurred to the reader that in a big climax of thunderous chords on the pianoforte the man sitting at the piano can hardly hear the singer at all above the general din he is creating? Think of it – it is delightful for the accompanist, but members of the audience sitting on the stage, as they sometimes do, will get a similarly uneven balance without enjoying it quite so much as the pianist does. The singer directs his voice away from the accompanist into the hall. The accompanist has therefore to use his discretion to ensure that to the bulk of the audience the tone of the voice and the pianoforte are of equal weight. If a *fortissimo* is marked, he must play *fortissimo*, although, as I said in a previous chapter, his standard of tone values will depend on the song and the singer's voice. A soprano with only an average-sized voice can stand a much bigger amount of tone from the pianist than a bass singer with a huge voice. In Mozart's "Allelujah" the accompanist can let himself go without fear of covering the soprano voice, but in the big climaxes in the "Volga Boat Song" the accompanist must be very discreet, or he will drown the bass singer completely. Again, in *forte* passages, the singer with a good-sized voice may have certain notes which are weak. They may be low notes, or they may come in the middle of the voice, or they may be notes sung to a vowel on which it is difficult to obtain a big tone, like the French "tu" or the German "ü". In these awkward places the accompanist, although instructed on the score to play *fortissimo*, tempers his tone. All these points must be watched and weighed carefully in rehearsal, because singers, for some strange reason, object to being drowned. The pianist cannot afford to be so public spirited as the famous conductor who on being accused of having drowned the singers with his orchestra replied: "I know, I did it intentionally, and thought that by doing so I had done a public service."

All the same, the accompanist must not, in his anxiety to be merciful to the singer, let his playing lose vitality and dynamic strength. A good singer likes to hear a mighty *crescendo* rumbling underneath him. The forceful playing of an introduction where the mood is white-hot will mean a lot to the singer. He will not feel he is fighting single-handed. If the singer has a small voice, however, and attempts to sing Frank Bridge's "Love Went a-Riding" the *fortissimo* of the pianoforte introduction must be tempered accordingly. The accompanist draws attention to the smallness of the voice if he plays his opening bars thunderously and suddenly reduces his tone to a whisper when the voice comes in. The playing, as I say, need not lose its vigour – it is only the general scale of volume which must be reduced. Vladimir de Pachmann, the great player of Chopin, was never able to produce a big tone, but you did not realize this because his scale of tone values was so extraordinarily fine. His *pianissimo* was such a whisper that his *fortissimo* sounded enormous by contrast.

These different questions of phrasing, balance, rhythm, &c., do not crop up one at a time. Consciously or unconsciously the accompanist has to deal with them all at once, in the same way that a man trying to hit a golf ball puts into one swing countless instructions that have been dinned into him by the professional.

Let me repeat that the accompanist wants the audience in the body of the hall to hear the voice of the singer and the voice of the piano in equal quantity. It follows inevitably therefore that from his piano stool he will hear his own tone more clearly (more loudly) than the singer's tone. This is frightening, but it is true.

I recommend any person who wants to accompany well to play for as many singers as he can, rather than confine himself to working with one singer, because with each different singer these problems will have to be dealt with anew, and in the light of experience the accompanist will cope with some of them automatically. The more singers he accompanies, the more ways he will find to his astonishment there are of interpreting one song. On the other hand, the more singers he associates with, the less frequently will he be caught at a disadvantage.

An accompanist with experience can assess in a few bars the musical and artistic resources of a singer. He can judge the size of the voice and its quality, whether the singer is sound rhythmically and musically, whether the singer is erratic or dependable. The

With Nicolai Gedda.

busy accompanist's life is in one aspect parallel to that of the jockey. A busy jockey will travel all over the country to race-course after race-course, and he will have to ride horses he has never seen before. I am told that some of these fellows will mount a strange horse just before the race, and will assess its qualities and its short-comings during the preliminary canter from the paddock to the starting-point. Likewise, with experience an accompanist can after a few bars gauge the qualities and idiosyncrasies of a singer. In fact, to carry the simile further, he will soon know whether he is in for a flat race or must be prepared for a few jumps.

EXCHANGE OF VIEWS. – It is essential that the accompanist should know what is in the singer's mind, if the singer has fixed ideas. How he gains this knowledge is immaterial so long as he gets it. Playing a song through once with the singer may tell him all he wants to know, but if this fails they will have to discuss it. Their views may be far from identical. To the singer it may be a work that he knows intimately and has performed frequently, whereas the accompanist may be ploughing through virgin soil. Careful though he may have been, perhaps his preliminary work failed to show him all that is in the song. Possibly his conception is entirely wrong, possibly he has overlooked some highlight in the piano part, possibly the singer, listening as he sings for a certain effect in the accompaniment (of rhythm or of colour), does not hear it and is disturbed thereby. Whatever the case may be, the accompanist should be grateful for any advice or help the singer through his experience is able to give him. For it is well for him to bear in mind that with a new song – no matter how conscientious his own preparation may have been – he cannot say he knows a song until he has heard it sung.

Of course the boot may be on the other foot. It sometimes happens that an accompanist knows a song better than the soloist. He knows how it ought to go and if he intends to be helpful and to pull his weight he will not be backward in coming forward, and will tell his colleague what he knows. He is by no means fulfilling his role adequately if he agrees with everything or any-thing the singer does. This is a case where the customer is *not* always right, but if he is a customer of seriousness and sincerity he will welcome the accompanist's advice. In my experience the greatest artists are modest people and simple to deal with – it is unnecessary to waste their time paying them puerile compliments. They are direct in their discussion with the accompanist, and the latter need not mince words with them if he has anything constructive to say. If they are singing out of tune – he should say so; if their rhythm is at fault – he should say so; and if he has any new light to throw on the song – he should tell them. There are many fine artists with whom I regard it as an honour to be associated, but they do not feel they are humbling themselves when they say to me: "Watch me carefully in this passage as I am inclined to hurry – hold me back"; or: "I am apt to drag here – don't let me do it." But as I say, great artists are like that.

There are some singers, however, who know everything, and these are the birds that need watching. They will hate being corrected, they will resent being advised. Nevertheless, the accompanist must steel himself and go to it. True, this type of singer may not forgive such an attitude on the part of the accompanist, and the result may well be that he will engage another pianist for his next concert. And a good thing too.

This independent stand should not be adopted – let me make this quite clear – by a young accompanist still serving his apprenticeship. He needs work, he needs experience, and cannot afford to jeopardize his hopes of being re-engaged. To him I say – if your singer offends every canon of musical taste – suffer silently and store it up in your mind; profit by the other's mistakes. Try to stop him singing wrong notes by all means, but do not gratuitously tender your advice on interpretation. You will not have to suffer so much as I did when I started my career, for most singers of today have a much higher standard of musicianship than they had when I was a young man.

Everything in the garden is not invariably lovely between two experienced artists, for discussion can become heated and relations strained. I remember a world-famous prima donna saying to me when rehearsing Wolf's "Ich hab' in Penna" (My Lover from Penna), "Finish the song with a chord where the voice part ends." I must explain that after the voice has finished there are nine bars of the most brilliant and glittering pianoforte writing – taking just over ten seconds to play. It is not too much to say that this piano postlude is the climax of the song. It was a joy to play and I took pride in it. Her wishes were not only a blow to me personally, but if they had been carried out they would have ruined the song. She refused to sing the song unless I cut off these nine bars. I refused to make the amputation. The long and the short of it was that the song was eliminated from the programme.

The accompanist is not always so blindly obedient as many people believe.

ENCORES. – The accompanist's advice will be frequently sought as to the choice of encores for a recital programme, and the singer at the last rehearsal will generally bring half a dozen songs from which the most suitable are chosen.

Audiences, however, do not invariably confine their enthusiasm to the end of a group when the artists are leaving the stage; possibly a song in the middle of the group will catch their fancy and they will applaud vigorously in the hope of hearing it again. Whether or not the singer complies with the audience's demand to hear a song twice depends on the type of song. Some artists have an unerring instinct over this. If it is a serious one they will not repeat it; they will rightly feel that its atmosphere could not be recaptured. They will also refuse to repeat a song which has strained their physical power or technical resources, knowing well that it could not be sung with such success a second time.

A less-experienced artist will often turn to the accompanist for advice when the audience puts him in this quandary. "Shall I repeat it?" he will call out, above the applause. The answer generally is, "No," though exceptions can be made of songs which are light and gay, and require, moreover, no effort to sing.

BY THE time he has rehearsed fifteen or twenty songs the accompanist will have a good deal on his mind. The exact tempo of each song and the new points which his colleague has helped him to discover must be memorized. Immediately after the singer's departure is the time when it is wise for the pianist to go over the whole programme he has been working on – while his memory is

still fresh. He should read through his music away from the piano –
as a conductor reads his score. The decisions the singer and he have
made will thus be "set". To remember the exact shade of tempo of
every song is difficult, particularly after only one rehearsal. But in
nearly all songs there is some phrase which provides the clue to
the pace, a phrase which can only be taken at *one* tempo. It may
not be the opening phrase, it may come in the middle of the song
and this "key phrase" must be searched for if there is any doubt as
to the tempo. If I, for instance, were uncertain what tempo I ought
to establish in "Linden Lea", by Vaughan Williams, I should
sing – under my breath – the last line of the verse:

And there for me, the ap-ple tree Do lean down low in Lin-den Lea.

This would certainly give me the "key" to the song's basic
tempo. But when I play Schubert's "Doppelgänger" (Shadow
Double) I sing under my breath, during the piano introduction,
the singer's opening phrase – the first line of the poem "Still is the
night".

Still ist die Nacht es ru-hen die Gas-sen

There is only one tempo – one true tempo – for this song and the
accompanist is bound to get it if he adopts these tactics.

It is imperative for him to get the tempo of each song firmly
fixed in his memory, as in most cases he may have to establish this
tempo in a lengthy introduction with the singer standing by
helpless to do anything, except fume inwardly, as I have shown
already.

With Elizabeth Schwarzkopf.

SOME SINGERS think it helpful to have one of their rehearsals in the concert hall. I do not think there is much to be gained by doing this, since the acoustics of a hall when empty are quite different to the acoustics of a well-filled hall. The audience constitutes a splendid sound absorbent without which the sound would echo and reverberate. If singers and accompanists hope to be able to gauge the amount of tone required to fill the place by singing or playing in the empty hall they will be disappointed; this will have to be done at the performance.

However, I do think that some comfort can be gained by visiting the hall before the concert and having a look at it; that is, of course, if the place is strange to one. Singers will want to see the size of it; accompanists will want to run their fingers over the piano. A first-class solo pianist has his own instrument with him wherever he goes, or at least always has the same make of piano to play on, but an accompanist has to take pot luck and use whatever piano he finds; this calls for a certain amount of adaptability. Splendid thoroughbred pianos, whose names are a guarantee in themselves, have individual qualities varying in accordance with their make, and each will have to be treated differently as regards touch; but often enough the unfortunate accompanist finds himself playing on a piano which can only be described as a crossbreed, as a mongrel.

I remember travelling to a concert in the North of England with a violinist to play three Sonatas with him. "I played," he said, "these sonatas last night with X" (mentioning one of the world's greatest pianists). With some anxiety I went on arrival at the town, straight to the hall. The piano was old and very tired and of no known breed. The contrast between my playing on this tin box and the great pianist on his superb instrument the night before can be imagined. I was reminded of a friend of mine who was serving in the 1914–18 War. Hearing that he was a famous violinist, a Tommy one night in the canteen pressed a fiddle into his hands with only one string to it – the "G" string – and said, "Give us the 1812 Overture, mate."

This enthusiast would have felt no awe, been not one whit surprised if the violinist – by some magic – had produced the sound of a full orchestra: chimes, cannon, and all.

FIVE

The Artists' Room

NERVES. – This sub-heading must not deceive the reader into supposing that this chapter is to be a scientific dissertation on a subject far beyond the powers of the writer. Nerves, however, must often enter into the calculations of an accompanist: the effect nervousness will have on him is worrying enough, but he must also be concerned for unrehearsed effects that nerves will have on an inexperienced partner.

A singer with an established reputation, particularly if he is a fine artist (reputation and artistry do not always go hand in hand), will be worthy of the occasion; he will put into the performance all that he promised at rehearsal, with the addition of that extra ounce of inspiration, excitement and fire that contact with a responsive audience gives him. He will be nervous, of course, but his nerves will be under control and therefore his concentration will not be affected. Such a singer gives the accompanist no qualms, as his work before the public is better than at rehearsal. One anticipates with the keenest pleasure accompanying such an artist.

I would not be so foolish as to infer that the accompanist is not nervous before a concert. I, personally, like to be, and feel there is something wrong if I am not. Without nerves or keen anxiety, my playing would be even duller than usual, but if I am frightened it is a bad business and means that I am improperly prepared for the concert and shall be a poor prop for an inexperienced singer, or an unworthy partner for a fine soloist. Concentration helps to dispel fright. The accompanist is lucky in that his eyes can be fixed on the score and on the keyboard, and that in the main he does not have to bother his head about showmanship. I say in the main advisedly, for this is an aspect of his work which must be considered as I shall show later.

It is delightful, of course, if what the prophets would describe as "fair weather" is expected. What happens when the accompanist's instinct tells him that there are storms ahead? What is he to do with the singer who is so overawed by the importance of the occasion that he is dithering with fright, sick with nerves? This person he instinctively feels will not only forget all the schemes that were laid at rehearsal but may become so "gaga" as to forget his notes or his words, to muddle his entries, to let his rhythm go all to pieces. Now truly the accompanist has cause to be nervous; but now, above all, is the time when he must be as steady as a rock. On an occasion like this the accompanist must be the "strong man" of the party and his success in steering his erratic partner through the chaotic time ahead may well depend on the thoroughness with which he, the accompanist, has prepared himself for this particular programme.

In the Artists' Room before the concert he must not show the slightest sign of nerves; in fact, if he has any doubts or misgivings he should conceal them. His demeanour and nonchalance may help to pull a shaking, inexperienced singer together. Eventually, if he is acting his part well he will hear the singer utter the time-worn words, "You are lucky people, you accompanists; you never get nervous."

A fussy or erratic singer can easily unsettle an accompanist who is unsure of himself. Therefore, he must not become worried if this singer, at the very last moment before emerging on to the platform, says something like this: "I was turning the programme over in my mind this afternoon, and my ideas about so and so have completely changed. It suddenly struck me that we should – &c., &c." This sort of thing used to upset me at one time, but now I let it go in at one ear and out of the other. These famous "last words" are rarely of much importance, and the accompanist need not bother his head about them. After all, singer and pianist have had several days and several rehearsals in which to turn the programme over in their minds, and for the singer to have suddenly

[67]

"seen the light" while he was taking his siesta earlier in the day is a little too much. He will forget his new idea, anyway, when he is before the public.

I remember once having to play for about four singers and a violinist at one of those interminable concerts that are intended to last for three and a half hours. One of the singers drew me on one side in the Artists' Room and said: "You understand, Moore, that *I* must be the success of the concert." I still wonder what this man wanted me to do to the other artists (incidentally his wife was singing on the same programme), but here was another instance of a "last word" which had to be ignored.

I very rarely fuss or worry in the Artists' Room, for fear of undermining the singer's confidence in me. It is no help to the singer to betray signs of nervousness. If the accompanist wishes to compose his mind he can gaze on the music, particularly the first group of songs, but he should not practise any of it on the piano in the Artists' Room, especially in the presence of his colleague; it is too late for that. All he should do is to look quietly through it. Also he should get a programme and make sure that all the songs are in their correct order and that he knows how to find each song without having to search for it. If the group consists of songs necessitating the use of three or four volumes it is a good system to write the volume and page number of the second song at the end of the first song, the volume and page number of the third song at the end of the second song, and so on. (Of course, at the performance, the singer and the accompanist not only make sure that both are ready to start, but one will whisper to the other the title of the next song, so that both of them *do* get to work on the same song.)

At one time I preferred at a concert to turn over the pages for myself, but I have had one or two unfortunate accidents which now lead me to ask for some kind of assistance in this matter. Concert platforms are draughty places, and some gremlin or impish elf – when there is no one beside me – gets to work and after I have turned the page, gently wafts it back again: I have had to puff like a grampus at the offending page in an effort to blow it back into place while my two hands were busily engaged on the keys. The page-turner should be informed in advance of the repeats or turnings back, if any, but only one group at a time should be shown to him, so that he does not get muddled, for he may not have seen any of the music before.

Sometimes the presence of this assistant is disturbing. He is, perhaps, totally insensitive to atmosphere. At the end of that lovely Richard Strauss song "Morgen" (Tomorrow) with the singer perfectly still, the pianist's hands motionless, the audience reluctant to disturb the peace by applauding, this busybody of a page-turner will be shuffling his feet and the music and making distracting movements as he looks for the next song. I have acquired the habit, therefore, of warning this kind person not to start searching for the music. "There is plenty of time," I say, "for me to find the music myself during the applause." In intimate songs, such as the cycles of "Winterreise", "Die Schöne Müllerin", or "Dichterliebe" I prefer to turn the pages myself.

Fussiness must be avoided. A fussy accompanist will fidget any singer and positively upset the nervous one. I feel a list of "do nots" might be helpful to the young accompanist. It is the product of my own painful experiences.

Do not rush into the Artists' Room and bombard your colleague with questions. For instance, *do not* say: "Will you give me the tempo of this song, so that I am quite sure about it?" This will tell the singer quite plainly that the accompanist either has the jitters or was sleeping during rehearsals.

Again, *do not* say: "Yesterday you felt you had a cold coming on, and I am wondering if you will be able to take your top notes *mezza voce* or not. Perhaps I had better be prepared for you to take them *forte*?" This is a question which the singer cannot answer until he has been on the platform.

Do not go into the Artists' Room and say you are tired. If your singer asks you how you are, you must answer, "Fine." You may be wracked with lumbago, have shooting pains in the head, have a touch of indigestion, and be limping with an in-growing toe-nail, but to any questions concerning your well-being, your invariable answer is, "Fine."

A friend of mine once talked too much. He was the leader of

an orchestra and shared the Artists' Room with the conductor. For the sake of something better to say, the conductor asked the leader how he was. My friend replied: "Do you know that after our three-hour rehearsal this morning I went straight home and have been teaching ever since. I am whacked."

He dropped into an arm-chair. The conductor was furious. He complained to the management, and asked them what sort of concert would it be when his leader arrived exhausted? Thus we may crawl on all fours in an exhausted condition to a concert, but we must walk into the hall as if we are as fresh as paint.

Do not at any time relate how wonderfully so and so sang these songs when you played for him last year. It will not help your singer, far from it; and he will not love you for it.

And finally, as you walk on to the stage, *do not* step on the soprano's train.

SIX

Performance

THE FIRST SONG. – At the risk of shattering the reader's illusions I must tear aside the veil of mystery which shrouds the god-like figures of musicians, and state that when they walk on to the platform they are often so petrified with nerves that they would give half their fee, or nearly half, to be elsewhere. It is natural that they should be in an excited (we hope not delirious) condition. If they are experienced artists neither will be badly shaken if the other does something which is not quite "according to plan" in the first song. I have noticed when accompanying a good musician that should I adopt a tempo in my introduction which is a fraction too slow, or a fraction too fast, he will not abruptly adopt a different tempo when he starts to sing; he will fall in with me and gradually ease me into the tempo he wants.

The accompanist can perform the same service for the singer. The latter may have taken too slow a tempo, there will be perhaps a long phrase in the song which must be sung in one breath; it will, the pianist knows, be a physical impossibility to cover it at this speed, and so the accompanist gently urges a slightly more forward moving gait, to which the singer instantly responds. Whether the singer accommodates himself to the pianist or the pianist to the singer, it can be done so gently that the audience cannot hear the machinery creaking – the grinding as we change gear. The proviso always being that I, the accompanist, am on the alert.

This reminds me that in a broadcast some time ago, I finished my talk on accompanying by saying these words: "And one thing more – sit on the very edge of your seat." I hissed these words with what I thought at the time truly dramatic effect. My meaning was more metaphorical than literal; it was that a would-be accompanist must be constantly on the alert while he is at the piano and was not an allusion to the physical motions he goes through in order to place his person on the piano stool. My parting words worried several enthusiastic listeners who wrote to ask me how I sat down. As I am punctilious with letters, I naturally informed them.

The singer as a rule likes to open his programme with a straightforward type of song requiring a healthy amount of tone, a song which will warm his voice without demanding the finest shade of *pianissimo*, or the loudest climax. It will therefore be a song which does not call for over much emotional or dramatic feeling. If he chooses such a song he is wise, for it will enable him to judge the acoustic properties of the hall. It will allow him to devote his mind to questions of tone and tone values without having to plunge in cold blood into the deeper waters of interpretation. This suits the accompanist admirably, for he has the same questions to answer, plus the balancing of his tone with the singer's. It will be remembered that I have said before, the accompanist can master this problem of balance only by experience.

In some halls you get the strange sensation that you are producing no amount of tone at all; it is as if there were a vacuum cleaner at the back of the audience, which sucks all the sound away from you. The singer and accompanist may believe – because they cannot hear themselves as effectively as they did in the studio – that the audience cannot hear them. In trying to overcome this sensation of impotence, they force their voice or thump their piano. This is a fatal mistake. If their well-produced tones fail to carry, their forced tone will carry even less – besides, it will put out of focus their plan of dynamics so carefully thought out at rehearsal. The man who drives a golf ball off the tee with an easy, smooth swing will get more length and accuracy than the man who uses brute strength. In the Royal Albert Hall I have heard singers, violinists, and pianists who could fill that vast place with a *pianissimo* tone.

Of course the *pianissimo* was well produced. I say then to the inexperienced singer and accompanist that the principles of tone quality and production which they evolved in the privacy of their studio remain the same for a large auditorium. If at first they find that their tone seems lost, they must take a firm mental grip on themselves and wait till they feel "at home". I am aware that this is easier said than done, but there is nothing else they can do about it. With each succeeding public appearance they will find they need less and less time to settle down. Nothing can teach them but their own experience.

At the end of the song the accompanist waits for the applause to begin and then finds the next song.

While the singer is still bowing to the public the accompanist is looking at this next song and getting its mood and its tempo into his head.

An unpleasant mannerism in which some accompanists indulge is that of idly strumming between the songs. Occasionally a singer will ask him to do this, and he gracefully complies with this request, but it is a bad habit. For one thing this strumming gives the ears of the audience no rest; they are not quite sure when they hear the piano whether they need or need not pay attention to the platform. They are quite content to look at their programme in peace and see what is coming next, without having their ears massaged by an unctuous murmur from the pianoforte. This strumming, too, will very quickly bring everybody down to earth with a bump; their imagination or their mood is rudely disturbed. When I say "everybody" I mean "everybody", save the pianist. And his strumming patently advertises the fact that he is quite insensitive and has no illusions.

While I am on this subject I might mention the playing of a chord which a singer often requires when there is no pianoforte introduction, so that he can get his note. This would be required in Schubert's "Heidenröslein" (Hedgerose) and should be indicated by a simple chord or *arpeggiando*, the former preferably. The singer may want his note at the top of the chord where he can hear it clearly, or he may be content with an inversion of this chord, but in either case the accompanist should play it softly and without flourishes. He should, in fact, exercise his proverbial talent for unobtrusiveness, and need not advertise that he is giving the singer his note. It is sometimes possible to communicate this note to the singer by surreptitiously sounding it softly while the applause for the preceding song is going on.

SHOWMANSHIP. – When good artists enjoy themselves in their music-making as much as the audience in their listening, you can depend on it those artists are playing or singing at the top of their form. There will be a zest and freshness in their work which quickly communicates itself to the listener. Toil and worry have been left behind in the studio.

One of the many things we admire in a great conductor is the ease with which everything he touches is accomplished. His hard work was all done at rehearsals. We lesser mortals can learn a lot from that, although technical difficulties as far as we are concerned are bound to obtrude more than we care to admit, and sometimes prevent us delivering the message entrusted to us by the composer. Our listeners, however, must not be aware of strain, or they will get anxious too. They would feel like the man who is motoring with an erratic driver. He dare not take his eyes off the road, he cannot gaze tranquilly at the scenery, he is too occupied in driving the car from the back seat. It is the same with our audience. We do not want them to become nervous, and so they must not be taken completely into our confidence. They must be deceived. We must not allow them to be aware, if we want them to enjoy the music, that we are overcoming (or attempting to overcome) technical difficulties.

And this is what I was referring to when I spoke of showmanship in a previous chapter. The audience will not enjoy an accompanist's playing of Strauss's "Ständchen" (Serenade), no matter how charmingly it is played, if he crouches low like a gorilla over the keyboard with his eyes glaring and his teeth clenched. He must not let his hearers know it is difficult, and should sit upright at the piano with hands, arms, and body relaxed and with facial muscles relaxed too, to avoid grimacing. Thus the audience's eyes will not be drawn from the singer. Please note that I do not suggest that the pianist play this song wearing an inane grin, as this again would attract undue attention to himself. The singer has to do the smiling,

With Victoria de los Angeles.

even though he, or she, may not feel like doing so. The fewer eccentricities the accompanist has, the better; he will not smile blandly during Schubert's "Der Tod und das Mädchen" (Death and the Maiden), nor will he look doleful while playing Strauss's Serenade. Difficult though the latter may be, the impression must be conveyed that it is executed with the greatest of ease. The audience that applauds the dexterity of a juggler is not aware that he is perspiring profusely under his immaculate top hat, that he is cursing copiously under his breath, or that he has practised some particular trick for months before venturing to perform it in public – it all looks so easy. The accompanist must give the same impression in songs which are carefree and joyous. In this category I put Schubert's "Musensohn" (Son of the Muses), Schumann's "Aufträge" (Messages), Wolf's "Er ist's" (It Is Spring), Brahms's "Frühlingstrost" (Spring's Solace), all of great difficulty, demanding accuracy and dexterity.

On the other hand, it does not do to look nonchalant in songs of dramatic intensity, no matter how easily the pianist may be able to overcome their difficulties.

Absorption in the words should prevent this. In "Die Wetterfahne" (The Weather Vane), "Der stürmische Morgen" (Stormy Morning), or "Mut" (Courage), three difficult accompaniments from Schubert's "Die Winterreise" ("Winter's Journey") cycle, he must look as if his heart and soul were in it. The audience likes to see that he is working hard in such songs.

Schubert's "Erlkönig" was ruined by one insensitive pianist. He made it obvious to the listeners that he was more concerned in letting us know how *easily* he could play his exhausting and formidable part than he was in the poem. In consequence, the drama of the ballad – hard though the singer strove – was dissipated. Schubert, Goethe, the singer and the audience had wasted their time.

This question of one's attitude at the piano may appear trivial to the reader, but it is of importance to the singer and the accompanist, and especially in songs where – to use a trite expression – an "atmosphere" has to be created in the piano part. Such a song is "Morgen" (Tomorrow) by Richard Strauss. With this song's

[76]

mood of complete peace and tranquillity, the accompanist in his twelve slow bars of introduction has to create the mood. We know he must play it beautifully and tenderly, but is that enough? Not if his attitude at the piano is a disturbing one. He wants the audience to appreciate the utter stillness of the whole song from the very first note he plays – therefore utter stillness must prevail on the stage. Any movement of singer or pianist will have a disturbing effect, and will ruin the picture they are trying to paint. They should wait a long time before starting this song, and the accompanist's hands should be on the keys, waiting there until the audience is ready. The singer will stand as still as a statue, perhaps with her eyes closed during this pianoforte introduction. Once started, the accompanist must make no unnecessary movement, no nodding of the head, or graceful passes in the air with his hands. The fingers must crawl over the keys and the body must be moveless. The head must be in a position where he can glance at the music or the piano keys without having to move it up and down. When the song is finished, he should remain in the same position with his hands on the keys until the tone has completely died away. This physical attitude of concentrated stillness will focus the audience's attention, as well as his own. The audience would be conscious, even if they were listening with closed eyes, of any movement on the stage in a song of this sort. Schubert's "Wanderers Nachtlied" (Wanderers' Night Song) and Brahms's "Feldeinsamkeit" (Alone in the Fields) would come under this heading, and the reader will have no difficulty in thinking of many more.

My oft repeated claim – that the singer and accompanist are, artistically speaking, equal partners, and my contention that the accompanist must so comport himself that, should the eyes of the audience stray towards him, he looks in the picture of a song – must not give a false impression. It is the singer who is mouthing the words of the poet. It is he whose face has to reflect the varying moods of the song. The audience's eyes should be on him. Their ears, however, should be equally open to the voice and the piano. They should listen to the two instruments as equally and impartially as they listen to the four voices in a string quartet. I am sure that a considerable percentage of the average audience does

[77]

not do this at a song recital. The voice and piano are to them separate entities, and their ears listen to one instrument only – the voice. They exclude the accompaniment not only from their consideration, they actually do not receive it, do not hear it. They are physically deaf to the accompaniment. They miss half the significance of the song in this way. The difficult piano accompaniments which do sometimes attract attention to themselves are generally of less aesthetic value than the simpler sounding ones.

PERFECT PARTNERSHIP. – The work of the accompanist is exhilarating when he is associated with a fine artist, and it is inspiring when he plays with one of greater artistic stature than himself. Each gives the other something psychologically. It is very hard to define this. There will be a real telepathic *rapport* between them which is sharpened by their mutual admiration and artistic agreement. A violinist or a singer is helped by the accompanist's genuine enthusiasm, and receives from that accompanist something which amounts to more than a beautifully played accompaniment.

The accompanist thrives on similar thought waves coming from the soloist. You may call it a mutual admiration society, but from these artists you will hear rare flights of imagination, you will hear real music. Each inspires the other, each eggs the other on. They will do things at performance which did not happen at rehearsal; an extra intensity of feeling will come into their work. It will have more fire, more tenderness, more excitement, and more repose. Their plans will not be upset, only improved upon, yet neither partner will be taken by surprise. They toss the ball from one to the other. Each listens to the other. One kindles a fire which the other helps fan to a blaze, each will be on his mettle and try to match his partner.

The accompanist will strive to whisper on his instrument, to reduce his tone to the same wisp of sound as the violinist, and he will seek to echo the tear-choked retrospect in the singer's voice. He will try to put the same passion into his playing. Each thinks at the performance in terms of the first person plural, each thinks not of a voice, or a piano, but of music. That is the true spirit of ensemble.

PULLING A SINGER THROUGH. – A fine singer and accompanist will undoubtedly help one another by throwing hints, and even on occasions a lifeline, in such a subtle way that no one but themselves knows it. (Evidence of this sort of thing was given me by a singer who said to me at a concert: "I am always afraid of forgetting my words, so keep the words firmly fixed in your brain. I am sure I shall remember them if you do this."

With an unevenly matched pair, however, this rapport does not exist. It may be that the singer does all the giving and gets nothing back from the accompanist. The singer may be able to soar vocally, but not spiritually. He will be earthbound by his partner. This, I assert categorically, is the usual state of the poll and is the *raison d'être* for this little book.

I am more concerned here naturally when the onus is on the accompanist, when it is he who has to do all the giving, when it is he who has to pull the singer through. If the singer is inexperienced and is uncertain of himself, the accompanist is the life-saver.

The most glaring and obvious instances, for example, are when the singer through a lapse of memory – and this can happen to the best of them – omits a large chunk in the middle of a work. He has jumped high and far. He will be sadly shaken when he lands, but the accompanist can catch him and see that he lands on his feet. This type of accident happens when a passage comes twice in a song. It turns off to one direction the first time we meet it, but to an opposite direction the second time we come to it. The singer may take the wrong turning; if the accompanist knows the geography of the song he will know exactly to which spot the singer has leapt, and will leap with him. The fact that the song is spoilt does not mean that the accompanist's interest should evaporate. He wants to save the singer, and he wants the audience to enjoy themselves, if it is at all possible.

Of course the song will be ruined to those people who are cognizant of what is going on. But the leap can be accomplished smoothly if the accompanist is alert. The knowing listeners will be taken by surprise and will "come to" and ask themselves what happened only when they hear the rest of the audience applauding. And the rest of the audience *will* applaud if the accompanist is able to cover up his partner's error, effecting a neat join by not reducing his tone or allowing any tentativeness to creep into his playing.

It is advisable for the accompanist not to exhibit a bewildered countenance or boggling eyes to the audience while this disaster is being enacted. For it is a disaster of the first magnitude, and though it may happen rarely I cite it only as an example of the more obvious form of life saving on the concert platform. After such an experience the singer will have aged visibly, while the accompanist will have those circles under his eyes which the ignorant attribute to dissipation.

Much less obvious mishaps can occur, however, which the accompanist may prevent or camouflage. The singer may have to be prodded occasionally. There may be a time when the singer is slow in getting on with a *crescendo*. I do not mean slow in regard to tempo, but slow in applying the ginger. This is where the accompanist prods his partner by making his *crescendo* on the piano regardless of the singer; the latter will either respond or be drowned.

A sensitive accompanist can often tell just before it happens when a singer is going to forget his words or his entry. He is prepared, thanks to this forewarning, to give the singer time to collect himself again. He gives the singer time by making a *rallentando* between two vocal phrases, or by making a *firmata*. If the singer's reactions are quick, he will soon get on the rails again. He may even have time to scan his words, but if not the accompanist may actually have to sound the note that his partner has to sing.

In some songs he will not make a *rallentando*. He will even put in extra beats, keeping the accompaniment moving with his left hand and sounding the singer's note with his right. Only in the last resort if it is a case of the singer forgetting his words should the accompanist call out the words to him. This would make the catastrophe too obvious. There is always the possibility that a song will be saved if the accompanist is able to give the singer a chance to recover himself *by* himself. The point is that the accompanist must provide that chance. I have heard the subject of "camouflage" described as an art.

[80]

Prevention is better than cure, but in the case of intonation the accompanist has to hear that the singer is singing out of tune before he can start to attempt to correct it. He does this by getting more sharpness into his tone, so that his tone will penetrate to the singer's ears, over or rather through his voice. Perhaps one of the notes in the pianoforte harmony is the very note that the singer should be singing, and so he makes this note predominate. When this actual note is not written in the pianoforte part, he must add it in the treble clef, where it will pipe loud and clear for the singer to hear. If the latter is singing a quarter of a tone sharp, or a quarter of a tone flat, it will be an extraordinary feat on his part to continue to sing out of tune, especially if the accompanist plays the vocal line with him for the whole phrase. Once having seen the danger signal, the accompanist will continue to be on the *qui vive*, and will sound the singer's note from time to time.

Is it any wonder, in the circumstances, that the accompanist always plays with the music in front of him and never from memory? He cannot memorize the repertoire of every singer and instrumentalist with whom he comes into contact. And as we have seen, the soloist will feel a sense of security in knowing that the accompanist with the text in front of him can, in an emergency, steer him to safety or even prompt him.

A sensitive singer will need only the most delicate of cues from his partner. Indeed, they can be so delicate that even the singer himself, while profiting by them, will not be consciously aware of them. The less sensitive the singer, the more pointed and therefore the more obvious these cues will have to be.

I admit that all these various contretemps may sound very unprofessional and raw in the telling, but they happen far more frequently than the average listener knows. The fact that the latter is not always aware of them is in a good many instances due entirely to the ingenuity of the accompanist.

Every musician has some weak spot somewhere in his armour, and it is up to the accompanist to have gleaned from rehearsals the foibles and failings of his partner. Each singer will have a different weakness, and at the performance the accompanist will be on his guard against it.

[81]

From the foregoing remarks the reader will readily understand what I meant when I said the accompanist must be intimate with the geography of a song. He must have an eye for country, not only knowing in advance all the scenery and beauty spots to be pointed out, he must be aware of the sharp bends that lie ahead of him and the concealed turnings and built-up areas. In fact, if he keeps his eye glued to the road, the accompanist will not only avoid accidents and the hospital, but will steer clear of the work-house too.

SEVEN

Bad Habits

It is not my intention to gibe at or to belittle singers. If the reader gathers that impression from the foregoing remarks I hasten to correct it, for my happiest hours have been spent in working with singers.

We have been told by those who ought to know that the age of the golden voice, of the Caruso-like quality, has departed; I know nothing about that, but I make bold to say that the standard of musicianship among singers today is higher than it ever was.

A quarter of a century and more ago there were prima donnas who made fame and fortune by singing no more than half a dozen operatic roles throughout their entire career. There were tenors never at a loss for an engagement whose whole repertoire seemed to consist of a couple of dozen ballads. The singers of the present day have a vast field spreading before them. Their work embraces not only the music of their own mother tongue, but of Germany, France, Italy, Russia, and many more besides.

We know how splendidly some of our singers are equipped, and what fine musicians they are. It is therefore in no carping spirit that I have made allusion to the sins of omission and commission of some of them. There are naturally more mediocre musicians than there are first-class musicians, and it is with the former variety who are down in the valley or half-way up the hill that the younger accompanist spends most of his time. He gets a view occasionally, and sometimes even breathes the rarefied air, of the mountain-top, but most of his time will be spent at lower altitudes.

This constant change can be very unhealthy: contagious diseases abound the lower we go. We accompanists must not catch bad habits from bad singers.

The nearest that the singer and pianist can get to an ideal performance is to do exactly what the composer wants, yet sometimes the singer will require his partner to do something which is in flat contradiction to the composer's markings. He will want an accent where there should be none, he will make a *firmata* where it is not needed, and he will make a *rallentando* when it should be *a tempo*: he will be *forte* when he should be *piano*: he may sentimentalize when the mood should be *nobilmente*.

The list is by no means exhausted. The singer will swear with his hand on his heart and tears in his eyes that he does and always aims to do exactly what the composer has written. It is very awkward. If he sings it one way and the pianist plays it another way the result is chaotic. Discussion may be of no avail, but what is an accompanist to do?

At the performance he must be *with the singer*, but afterwards let him erase the memory of it from his mind so that the next time he tackles this piece of music his playing will not be tainted by this so-called interpretation.

Our love of a fine song must not be killed by the singer's inability or our own inability to cope with it.

The foregoing, let me repeat, does not apply to fine singers. A good artist, doing me the honour of scanning this little section on "Bad habits", should not take umbrage at what I have written, for my remarks obviously have no relation to him.

EIGHT

Sight Reading and Transposition

SIGHT-READING is like transposing – a matter of practice. The more sight-reading a young accompanist is forced to do, the better. I used to find that my sight-reading when alone in my studio was halting, and I would feel my way very gingerly through a new piece of music. This, I think, was because rightly enough I would not only read the notes but also try to observe every nuance, every detail, at the same time. Reading a new accompaniment through with a singer or a violinist at my elbow who knew the piece intimately, I found I would make a much better shot at it than I would have done alone. With a soloist carrying me along with him, I would go straight through the work from beginning to end, wrong notes or not, accidents or not. Together we would sweep clean through it. Sometimes chunks of notes would be missed, sometimes the composer's markings, but we would never lose the tempo. I was forced to do this kind of thing over and over again at rehearsals, and it was very good for me. Much better than sight-reading alone, when there would be nobody to drive me and keep me in the tempo. A good sight-reader is an expert skipper, he is aware that his fingers will be unable to grapple with all the notes when he is facing the music for the first time. His eyes, always a beat or two ahead of his fingers, will be suddenly confronted by an angry-looking cluster of notes like bees ready to sting him; or by a group of notes at each end of the keyboard supported or suspended by a forest of ledger lines, like spiders sneering at him. But his eyes cannot probe their mysteries or prove their identities; he has no time to track them down, for already his fingers are in the mêlée and his eyes are beyond.

If he were asked afterwards how he navigated these awkward passages he would reply that some of the notes had been abandoned or slurred so that he could keep the rhythmic pulse alive.

I have seen young players gazing morbidly at a new piece of music as if it had some horridly fascinating power over them. One would have to shake them, one felt, or they would become hypnotized. I have felt the same sensation myself. It is caused by the fear of striking wrong notes or making some other mistake, but, as I have hinted above, what do a few wrong notes matter so long as the rhythm is kept going?

When confronted by a new piece it is unnecessary to gaze at it for more than ten seconds before starting to play. This is time enough to see what key it is in, the number of beats to a bar, and whether the *tempo* should be slow, moderate, or fast. By all means let the pianist count when he starts to play, but under his breath, please.

TRANSPOSITION. – A good accompanist is expected to be adept at transposition. Frequently singers will ask him to put up or to put down a song a half tone, a whole tone, or more. This has been known to happen frequently just before emerging on to the concert platform. Sometimes their request is too much for the accompanist to comply with straight off. For instance, I was once asked at rehearsal to play "Nachtzauber" (Night's Magic) by Wolf, a tone down, and another time to play "Zur Warnung" (Warning) by Wolf, a tone up. I did not feel any sense of shame when I told the singer I should have to look at these songs by my-self for a little while. (A little while? I was flattering myself: the songs bristle with accidentals and unexpected progressions.) Singers are extremely reasonable as a rule about this sort of thing, and listen with tolerance to the first inaccurate attempt at trans-position, particularly if the interval they require to be transposed is a wide one. The Tonic Sol-fa system is used by many when training to transpose, and there are a good many text-books on this subject.

There are two other aspects of transposition, however, which I would like to dwell on. The songs I have mentioned, "Night's Magic" and "Warning", are difficult to *transpose*, but not to *play* once your brain is functioning in the new key. On the other hand, a song may not be difficult to transpose in terms of transposition, but it may be extremely difficult to *play* in any other key than its original. Any change of key in a fast-moving song will involve a change of fingering, and this new fingering is almost impossible to arrange without some little preparation.

We are told that Brahms was once playing the Kreutzer Sonata with a violinist. The piano was so flat that the violinist asked Brahms to transpose the whole sonata a half-tone higher, so that he would not have to tune the violin strings down. Only a giant such as Brahms could have accomplished such a feat, but I still wonder if he managed to play all the notes. If he did, it was a prodigious feat. Assuming that he did, the wonder of it lies in the physical facility which enabled Brahms's fingers and hands to adapt themselves to the different fingering and hand positions that the new key demanded, not so much in the fact that his brain was capable at a glance of seeing the whole piece in a strange key. Reading the Kreutzer Sonata away from the pianoforte, as we would read the newspaper, Brahms could have transposed the Kreutzer into any key. Many a good pianist today could *read* the Kreutzer and transpose it in his mind into A flat or A sharp, but to *play* it in those strange keys would be another matter; the notes would no longer be "under the hand".

Schubert's "Liebesbotschaft" (Love's Message) was originally written in the key of G for high voice. In this key the accompanist can make the little brook ripple softly and sweetly; his fingers literally flop into position with ease. But voices of a lower compass also want to sing this charming song. The *tessitura* of the original key being too high for them, the song is published in other keys, for example in E flat. But the mere fact that it is *printed* in the new keys is of little help to the accompanist, for he could have transposed it into any key. But the point is this, his hand no longer flops naturally into position; technically the song has become more difficult to play. Of course, the accompanist can "cover" the notes somehow, but can he make the song ripple as softly and as smoothly as it rippled in the original key? The song once easy must now be practised anew and refingered. And yet the audience is not aware of these difficulties that the accompanist has to overcome. They know only that for some unaccountable reason the brooklet has become a torrent and is thundering and heaving and bumping over the rocks. Unless, indeed, the accompanist addresses the audience thus: "Ladies and Gentlemen, that song was played in a transposed key, but I really can play it most beautifully in the original key, as you will hear if you come to this same hall on Thursday next." But we accompanists do not do that sort of thing; we suffer the "slings and arrows of outrageous fortune" silently. If you did but know it, we are martyrs, a noble band ready to sacrifice our comfort for the singers.

The second aspect of transposition applies more to quality of tone. Again it is a problem of which only the accompanist is aware. I can explain it best by recounting a personal experience. On successive evenings I was playing Rachmaninoff's song, "Spring Waters". The first evening it was for a soprano who sang it in the original key, and the second evening for a contralto in a transposed key. A friend who happened to be at both performances said how curiously lacking in sparkle and brilliance the song seemed in the lower key. If this was the case, other people in the audience knowing nothing about transposition, and caring less, must have thought my playing of it very dull, for I must admit the contralto sang it magnificently. I still think I was to blame for it. I should have contrived by some trick of touch or tone to make the song sparkle in the lower key, as it naturally did in the original key. Technically, I handled the accompaniment in the same way for the contralto as I did for the soprano, and that was where I made my mistake. This may sound unreasonable, but it is worth thinking about.

Similarly, a high voice will sing a song that is originally written for a low voice. Moving up to a higher key a song such as "Feldeinsamkèit" (Alone in the Fields) by Brahms, the accompanist must be on his guard against loss of profundity and sonority. Here a little more weight with his bass, and putting what little weight the right hand requires on to the *lower* notes of the chords, will be helpful.

[88]

We accompanists should not feel disgruntled that we have these difficulties to contend with, or complain that we are not given the indulgence of the listener. The critical music lover is listening to the performance on its merits; it is up to us to make the music sound convincing.

As a young man I was gifted with what is known as "perfect pitch", and this was an impediment rather than an advantage to me when I had to transpose: playing a piece of music in B flat when my eyes saw the printed page in C natural, upset my ears and brain, I found my fingers subconsciously wandering back to the tones I could hear with my inner ear – the tones that I saw on the printed page.

During my "perfect pitch" period, a singer with whom I frequently worked asked me to transpose a song down one tone from A flat to G flat. There was a top A flat at the end of the song, and he was frightened of it, so I undertook this transposition; having several hours to study it before our concert. It was not a very difficult change to make except for one stretch of some dozen or so bars in the middle of the song – bars of startling modulations which were crawling with pestiferous accidentals. At the performance I embarked on the transposed song with quiet confidence, but when I approached this dark forest of quick-moving double-sharps and double-flats I became nervous – in fact I lost myself. I beat and hacked my way through the undergrowth and got entangled. When I emerged breathless into the clearing I found, to my horror, that I was now playing the accompaniment not one tone *lower* but one tone *higher* than the original key. This nearly killed my colleague, for he now had to sing a top B flat instead of the G flat he had bargained for. A nasty guilty feeling still steals over me when I recollect his bulging eyes, swelling neck, and the awful noise he made as he flung himself, like a fish out of water, at a note that was beyond his reach.

This was the end of a beautiful friendship.

The gradual loss of perfect pitch has been an advantage to me as an accompanist, since it makes the act of transposing less hazardous for me – and for the singer.

With Daniel Barenboim.

NINE

Orchestral Accompaniments

ONE of the least grateful tasks which the accompanist has to perform from time to time is playing piano transcriptions of orchestral accompaniments. Singers like to sing operatic arias, violinists like to play concertos, but they cannot always have an orchestra to accompany them. The accompanist, frail though he may be, becomes a substitute for a hundred men.

Not being conceived in terms of the piano, most of these transcriptions are very unpianistic. "La donna è mobile" (Woman Is Fickle) from *Rigoletto*, "One Fine Day" from *Madam Butterfly*, or the Prologue from *Pagliacci*, do not present any great terrors to the accompanist, but they are not absorbingly interesting to play.

It is permissible in such arias as I have mentioned to enrich the accompaniments somewhat by enlarging the chords and by doubling the bass to ensure that the singer will get something approaching the support that he gets from an orchestra. This enriching and enlarging, however, should not be mere extemporization, but the result of knowledge of the orchestral score. This knowledge enables the accompanist to hear the orchestral tone in his imagination and he can then try to get the tonal effect of strings, woodwind, or brass into his playing. Of course, it is impossible to reproduce orchestral variety of tone on the piano, but a transcribed accompaniment sounds much richer if the pianist is familiar with the orchestration. In other words, he can be extravagant and splash a little.

Generally where operatic arias are concerned, the pianist need not be too pedantic or precious in his playing, and liberal use can be made of the sustaining pedal. To get the effect of brass, for example, it is obvious that nicety of touch must be thrown to the winds. The accompanist must fairly *dig* into the keyboard. (This, I must underline, is a special effect, and should be used on rare occasions only. It is ruination to good piano playing to make a habit of reproducing this brassy colour every time a *forte* or a *fortissimo* is demanded.) To get the effect of a full string tone the pianist would use weight *without* punch. The reader will have no difficulty in remembering passages in Verdi, Puccini, Massenet, &c., where the accompanist can literally throw his full weight about so that the listener is not too patently aware of the fact that the music really does need an orchestra. The Prologue from *Pagliacci* is a case in point.

The orchestral accompaniments of Mozart and Bach should not be subjected to this treatment. The piano transcriptions of Mozart's operatic arias and concertos lie beautifully under the fingers, and I feel when all is said and done that his music should be treated by the pianist with the refinement and style that it deserves.

Of all orchestral accompaniments by far the most difficult for the pianist are those to Bach's Cantatas. There is no question here of adding or enriching as I suggested in the Italian arias. There are far too many notes, and vital notes, too, for the technique of the pianist to encompass. The trouble here is to know which notes can be left out without anybody discovering it. If the pianist tried to play all the notes he ought to play, the long *legato* phrases which are the joy of this wonderful music would be jerked, bumped, and chopped about by the struggle his fingers were making to keep their appointments. No, these phrases must sound easy-flowing and natural. Therefore some of the notes must be sacrificed and the accompanist will not only have to practise hard at a Bach aria, he will also have to use great discernment in deciding what to leave out.

This is what many fine accompanists have to do, though they admit it with great reluctance. Their pruning is not, of course, done haphazardly but after much thought and to the end that Bach's line will flow freely and smoothly.

TEN

Folk-Song Accompaniments

THE orchestral accompaniment on the piano, with its justifiable elaboration, must not be confused with the discussion in this chapter.

Singers have frequently told me that young accompanists are very fond of embellishing a song accompaniment, that is to say, putting in notes that are not there. This is an indefensible vulgarity. It is hard enough to play the notes that are written as they should be played. Accompanists who indulge in this wild extravaganza do not know where to draw the line, for, dare I say it, there is something to be said for extemporizing.

The organist will take no liberties when he is playing the sonatas of Bach or Handel; it would be outrageous for him to do so, but he will be expected to decorate a hymn tune. As he accompanies the choir he will make a solo of the descant in one verse, in another he will get his choir to sing in unison, and alter the written harmony of the accompaniment to his own fancy. If he is a musician of taste, no one would object to this.

There is a parallel in the pianist's case. He commits an outrage, as I have said, if he tries to embellish a song. The overwhelming conceit which prompts this is beside the point; what matters is that the listener is overcome with nausea. If a composer must be murdered let the crime be committed in private.

A famous singer told me that he introduced "Erstarrung" (Numbness) from Schubert's "Winter's Journey" to a world-renowned virtuoso pianist and that "reading it at sight he improved on Schubert by playing the left hand in octaves instead of the single notes as originally written". I did not enthuse. He was a law breaker, in my opinion.

I think an exception can be made to this law in the accompanying of folk songs. No attempt should be made to embellish those folk songs which have already been arranged by masters such as Brahms, Bartók, and Vaughan Williams, &c., but often a volume of folk songs with eight or ten verses to each song will have space on the printed page for only one verse of piano accompaniment, and this, as likely as not, will be written in four-part block harmony. Surely it is unreasonable to plod flat-footed through this song with no variation other than a *forte* or a *piano*.

The old Somerset song, "The Raggle Taggle Gipsies O", has no fewer than nine verses of dramatic narrative and declamation, and the accompanist is, I feel, entitled to differentiate between the wife's voice and the husband's voice, and portray as well as he can in his playing the gradually unfolding drama of the story. He can do this by some slight embellishment within the confines of the rhythmic pattern of the song, as well as by dynamics. We have heard this sort of thing done with sometimes amusing, sometimes dramatic effect by the accompanists of the B.B.C. men's chorus in excerpts from the Students' Song Book, and very acceptable it has been.

Having conceded this, I now practically withdraw it all with the comment that the accompanist who indulges in this fantasy must be an expert.

Once again I must remind the reader that in my opinion extemporization may be used for some folk songs, but for folk songs only (even this will be frowned on by many people), and has no relation whatever to the playing of strophic songs, by great composers which I referred to in Chapters 2 and 3.

With Leon Goossens.

ELEVEN

Piano and Violin Sonatas

So far I have only made passing reference to the accompanying of stringed instruments. I have postponed discussing this most important branch of our work, since it is more subtle and more difficult to write about. Naturally many of my comments on playing for singers are equally applicable to, and have a direct bearing on, our ensemble work with instrumentalists.

The musical meaning of a piece for violin or 'cello is generally less obvious than the musical meaning of a song. The words of a song make the meaning of its music clear, not only colouring the reading of the music but also making the composer's intentions unmistakable. It requires true and discerning musicianship, however, to get to the heart of the violin music of Bach, Mozart, Beethoven, Schubert, Brahms, &c., for such music has no programme to guide the performer.

No young accompanist should confine all his attention to singers and neglect an opportunity of working with a string player; he will find that this will call for even more sensibility than is generally required for a song accompaniment. He will find it more difficult to overcome problems of technique, tone colour, and balance in instrumental music, and especially in the playing of sonatas; an intimacy of musical understanding with his partner and a unanimity of attack are not so easily obtained. Much more practising and rehearsing will be needed.

The accompanist's work with the violinist is divided into two sections, sonata playing and the accompanying of small solo pieces. I will deal in this chapter with the former.

Nothing is more enjoyable than to partner a violinist in a piano and violin sonata. Many solo pianists have discovered this, and some of them are extremely good at it, but in my opinion the majority of them are so used to playing a lone hand, to going their own sweet way, that they do not make up the ideal team. Through the nature of his work the accompanist is better qualified than most solo pianists for ensemble playing: he is accustomed to *listen* to the other fellow.

MATCHING THE VIOLIN TONE. – The proposition of making the tone of the pianoforte match the tone of the violin seems an impossible and unreasonable one. How can the pianist hope to emulate the fiddle's sustaining power and its ability to increase and decrease the volume of a sustained note? Why, it might be asked, should he attempt it? To answer this, another book would be required and most certainly another author; but I can suggest a few reasons why this apparently hopeless attempt should be made. In the first place, the violin – a miracle of construction – has the most beautiful tone quality, and it makes the most satisfying sound, of all instruments. Again, it is capable of a *legato* which is the despair and envy of all players of the piano. I am not exaggerating when I say "despair".

This is my feeling when I am playing Grieg's Sonata in C minor for piano and violin, and I ask the reader to look at the second movement. The piano announces the theme, a slow, tender melody, and not until the forty-fourth bar does the violin make its entry, repeating melodically exactly what the piano has already said. Every time I have played this introduction and even, I must admit, when I have heard other pianists play it, it has always seemed cold and colourless compared with the warmth of feeling and velvet quality of tone which the bow has been able to woo from the violin. With the entry of the violin we are transported to a higher sphere. The pianoforte seems incapable of so much warmth and so much feeling. Yes, I feel a pianist can do much worse than attempt to match the string tone.

In slow, sustained music it is the percussive nature of the instrument which is the pianist's eternal trouble. The fiddler *draws* the tone from his instrument, but the pianist *strikes* the tone from his. The mere thought of *striking* the notes at once suggests the difficulty of making a pianoforte passage *legato*, for this passage, calling for dozens of tiny movements from the pianist's fingers, can be executed by one sweep of the violinist's bow. It seems to me that in music of a *legato* nature the idea of *striking* should be completely banned from the pianist's mental outlook. His tone must be *drawn* from the piano. The fingers, therefore, must not drop on to the piano keys, but be *placed* on the keys, depressed, and then drawn away.

This action I can best describe in the following manner: First put a dice or a nut on a table. Then spread your fingers and place the finger-tips lightly on the table all round the dice, but at a distance of an inch or more away from the dice so that it is covered by the palm of your hand like a tent. The wrist is held high. Now draw your fingers lightly towards the dice along the surface of the table without your wrist moving until your fingers grasp the dice and lift it clear of the table.

Not a felicitous illustration, but it is some such action as this that the pianist must employ to avoid percussion. One should try to play the opening bars of the César Franck violin and piano sonata in this way. The finger-tips need only be raised a quarter of an inch clear of the keys, and the sustaining pedal will hold the tone. For the pedal, of course, is essential where *legato* and tone production are concerned.

Once more I exhort the student to listen and listen again to the violin tone. It is only by using his ears that the quality of his tone will be improved. I make no apology for falling back on my old "stand by" the ear, or by naming the ear as the governing factor of the situation. I do regret, however, that I cannot be more explicit. The question of matching the tone of the piano to the *cantabile* tone of the violin is too subtle and complex for me to explain.

The easiest violin effect to imitate is *pizzicato* – the plucking of the strings. In the third movement of Brahms' D minor piano and violin sonata there is a short passage where the piano has the theme with the fiddle playing a *pizzicato* accompaniment. It is not impossible here for the tone of the piano to be almost identical with that of the violin, if care is taken to use little pedal and if the fingers are snatched off the keys as rapidly as the violinist's forefinger brushes his strings. A singularly enjoyable sensation it is to feel that the pianoforte is matching the violin's *pizzicato* tone here. But I still think that an attempt to do this should not be abandoned when the bow is drawn across the strings.

The pianoforte playing must be hammerless, that is all I can say.

B A L A N C E. – Like the singer, the violinist has a natural aversion to being drowned in a flood of piano tone, but he need have little fear of this with a good ensemble pianist. Of course, some discretion is required on the pianist's part in order to get a perfect balance, particularly when the violinist is playing on the lower strings. Soaring high on the "E" string in *forte* passages, the violin can stand plenty of volume from the piano. In the huge climaxes in the last movement of the César Franck Sonata, the composer several times asks for *fff*, and the pianist can obey this instruction without the slightest fear of covering the high violin notes.

The piano lid should always be raised on the short stick for sonatas. Violinists are mistaken when they imagine that they will not be heard so clearly with the piano lid open. If the piano were closed, the pianist would have to pound at it to get a *fortissimo*, the very percussive effect, in fact, that he so much desires to avoid. The same applies to *pianissimo* playing. If the lid is open the softest tones will have a carrying quality with the least possible pressure from the fingers, a lesser sense of percussion. Indeed, it is not impossible that pianoforte makers had this in mind when they constructed their instruments with a short stick.

T E C H N I Q U E. – Technical difficulties abound in sonata work. In the Beethoven sonatas, for instance, there are passages which you will be forced to practise as long as you live and then never feel quite certain that they will be perfect at performance. Whenever the Kreutzer Sonata is mentioned to me my mind leaps instantly to those notorious passages in the first movement, and a

With Yehudi Menuhin.

sickly feeling comes over me. (I refer to those passages in broken thirds and sixths with the hands in contrary motion.) Similarly unpleasant passages occur in Bach and Mozart and there is only one way to tackle them, and it is not by a correspondence course. It is by practising, slow practising.

I find it helpful to pencil my score with fingering, not necessarily writing the fingering for each note, but for one or two notes in a group of notes. Thus in a scale or arpeggio passage if the thumb has to pass under the fourth finger, I would write a large figure four on the music. This would stop me passing my thumb under the third finger and getting into a muddle. But these figures should be written boldly, not meanly, for the player may be nervous when approaching such a passage, and his wild, roving eye will pick up large figures clearly, especially if the copy is not littered with them. An occasional large figure will act as a guide post and will help to give a feeling of security. It is necessary to practise some passages so many times, in order to perfect them, that they will gradually lodge in the memory, and it is then that the merest glance at the music will suffice to pick up these guide posts.

UNANIMITY. – A sonata which I would say calls for all the qualities I have tried to enumerate is Beethoven's Opus 96 in G major. The piano part, like the fiddle part, is lyrical from beginning to end. One part weaves itself round the other in the most intimate interplay. It is the perfect example of the violin and piano duet; equal weight is wanted from the two instruments and, if possible, the same quality of tone. Above all, the players *must* each feel the same way over every note of it. Their views and intentions must be identical for each phrase and nuance. Sonatas such as the charming Grieg, the romantic César Franck, and the vigorous Beethoven Kreutzer call for this unanimity, but Beethoven's Opus 96 needs it in an even greater degree.

An intimate musical understanding between sonata players is required not only because it is essential that they both have the same broad conception of a work and that they both strive for the same ends; there is a much more prosaic reason. It is harder, the pianist will find, for them to be exactly *together*, to play as *one*, than it was when he was partnering a singer. The latter nearly always telegraphs to the pianist when he is moving from one note to the other by a change of vowel or by an intrusive consonant; also he is in the pianist's direct line of vision. Not so the violinist. True he changes from a down bow to an up bow and vice versa, warning enough for a pianist, even though it be a matter of a split second; but in most musical phrases he will have several notes to one bow, and this is where unanimity is not easily achieved and requires much rehearsing.

At the beginning of a movement the pianist will often have to turn his head so that he can see the violinist out of the corner of his eye in order to get a perfectly timed attack. This is not difficult if the violinist is starting with a down bow. He can make a slight downward movement with his fiddle as an indication, just as the leader of a string quartet does. Sometimes he will prefer to watch the motion of the pianist's right hand, especially if he, the violinist, is commencing with an up bow, when it is not so easy for him to make an indication. In either case a slight gesture is all that is wanted. One violinist with whom I was associated made such violent movements with his shoulders and his fiddle that he created a positive draught. It looked so bad, too.

TWELVE

Accompanying the Strings

THE equality in partnership between violin and piano in sonatas is unquestioned, but this equality does not obtain in the playing of violin solos, where the accompanist is often only expected to provide a background. The great composers of the past did not write small violin pieces with piano accompaniment. The sentimental or bravura violin solo was not their métier; they were only interested in concertos, and in duets for violin and piano in sonata form.

The tinkling or vamping piano writing to the violin pieces "Heyre Kati", "Zapateado", and "Ronde des Lutins" are fair examples of the little use that was made of the accompaniment prior to this century. If I appear to strike an attitude of superiority where these pieces are concerned, it is only here at my writing-table that I do so, for when I have to perform them I am aware that the very fact that they are easy makes it incumbent on me to execute them perfectly. It is taken for granted, and rightly so, that we pianists provide a flawless accompaniment to such pieces. We cannot afford, therefore, to let our vigilance slacken. These quick bravura pieces often find us lagging a fraction of a beat behind the fiddler, who has less reason than we have for taking it easy, and who will be very much on his toes. We should remind ourselves that it is our duty to anticipate all he does in order that we may walk, or gallop, or fly abreast of him. The sentimental piece which in our innermost hearts we may regard as sloppy will be improved and will be made interesting for us if we try to match the fiddle tone.

It is not until we come to the more modern composers that we find solo violin pieces with interesting accompaniments.

Fritz Kreisler, who has greatly enlarged the violinist's library of solo pieces, makes his piano parts pianistic and enjoyable to play. He evidently gave his accompaniments great attention, for they are plentifully strewn with accent, *staccato* or phrase marks. Even the simple Rondino (Beethoven–Kreisler) will repay a little attention. Every time the theme returns, the accompaniment, according to the instructions, should be treated in a different way. We are expected only to provide a background in this piece, but our variations of touch and accent should be apparent. This is typical of many of the Kreisler pieces.

Harking back to my remarks on being perfectly together, I can remember performances of Kreisler's "Caprice Viennois", in some of which I was participating, when the violinist and pianist were most certainly not playing as one man. The reader will doubtless remember the section of that piece with the lilting berceuse refrain.

The notes here are easy to play, but the ensemble is difficult. It is only after rehearsing that we can anticipate with certainty the rhythmic shape of the violinist's rubato and play together as one.

To me it seems that the more modern the composer, the more responsibility is thrown on the piano part. The piano in Szymanowski's violin solos is of equal importance to the fiddle. It would be too controversial to say that our task is more difficult in "La fontaine d'Aréthuse" than the fiddler's. Certainly the latter would disagree with me. Be that as it may, no one would deny that the accompaniment to this piece requires hours of practising. We are, in fact, the fountain and have to make our liquid cascades of notes shimmer like water in the sunshine. The performance of this work needs a pianist with an exquisite lightness of touch, perfect pedalling, and a good pianoforte. Perhaps in fairness I ought to add that it needs a good violinist too.

THE VIOLONCELLO. – In playing sonatas with or accompanying the 'cello, our predominating problem is that of balance. The 'cello, like the bass voice, can easily be overpowered by pianoforte tone. Our standard of tone values, therefore, must be readjusted. Nevertheless, many a time we shall find *fortissimo* marks in the piano part. How are we to treat them? We cannot ignore them, or be over-discreet and play softly while the 'cellist is digging away hugely on his C string, for our playing thus would sound mincing. The two splendid Brahms 'cello and piano sonatas present us with this difficulty. In the vigorous third movement of the E minor Sonata, where so much of the 'cello writing is on the lower strings, we have to avoid the alternative evils of drowning the 'cello by the thick pianistic writing, or of tickling the keys in a way Brahms never contemplated. The first alternative ruins the beautiful nature of the 'cellist, and the second ruins the character of the work. To avoid both evils it is best to play this movement with as little sustaining pedal as possible, for the abuse (which is another way of saying over-use) of the pedal is the cause of the piano tone becoming so thick and muddy that the 'cello tone cannot come through it. I would also suggest that you play this movement with a crisp, *staccato* touch, not on the surface of the keys, but with energetic finger action, so that your notes have clear articulation and substance. This is often the treatment you should give the piano part in pieces where the 'cello voice is singing in the same register as you are playing.

The Scherzo from Rachmaninoff's 'Cello Sonata should be handled in this way, for in this movement we are playing down in the bass in the same octave as the 'cello. When the 'cello is singing on the higher strings or playing in a much lower register than we are, then we need not be so fearful of drowning its tone. Some of its deepest bass notes, as found in Beethoven's A major Sonata, will sound clear and strong through the tone of the piano because the latter is playing high up in the treble, in a different sphere, as it were, to the 'cello.

A good example of this is found in that perfect specimen of 'cello writing, the Elegy, by Fauré.

The second subject of this work is announced on the piano.

This delightful passage continues for ten long bars (before the solo changes hands) with the 'cello playing a subsidiary part, and the 'cellist should be content to play his bass notes very softly. If he is a rococo type and plays too loudly he will force the pianist to increase his tone proportionately; dynamically it will all be thrown out of focus to the detriment of the music's mood.

With Jacqueline du Pré.

Conclusion

I WILL not bewilder the reader with a lengthy catalogue of the attributes that good accompanists ought to possess.

Do we need tact, that prosaic label which is so often attached to us? We need neither more nor less of it than anyone in any other walk of life.

Are we expected to be obedient, to obey without question the whims and caprices of whomsoever we are accompanying? I hope I have exploded that notion in this little book. I still pursue with unabated resentment a critic who, in the dim and distant past, assigned that doubtful quality to me.

Should we spend all our days and all our nights in being "sympathetic"?

But I could go on for a long time in this strain. These epithets are thrown at all accompanists occasionally. I personally can stand it if I only receive them one at a time, but if I were ever described as a "tactful, obedient, and sympathetic accompanist" I should feel that that was another and more polite way of calling me "worm".

The ensemble pianist or the accompanist or the man "at the piano" – to be first rate at his job does not need to be a superman. When I described him as a saint in an earlier page I was only alluding to his patience and long-suffering – to his beautiful nature!

He *does* need to be a good pianist, he *does* need sensitive ears, and he *does* need a sensitive musical brain.

Strangely enough, too, he *does* need in his chemical make-up, that repository of all human feeling, that source of poetry, fire, and romance, namely, a heart.

[111]

Afterword

DEAR GERALD,

I am writing to you with the imposing sweep of Wellington harbour glistening through the window of a hilltop house in Highbury . . . so English a name for a suburb and yet twelve thousand miles from Islington. It is a glorious summer dawn here and I hope that you and Enid, on the other side of the world, are cosily ensconced in Beechwood Cottage and beginning to think about a warming drink before dinner.

When I mentioned that I was lucky enough to be coming to New Zealand to escape part of the winter, you told me with a touch of the regret allowed to a seasoned and lively traveller, that your career had never brought you here. But then a great deal of your work was undertaken before the advent of this jet-age of mixed blessings which allows artists to hop from one end of the world to the other; (despite being high-flyers we accompanists are expected to retain in our minds the down-to-earth walking speeds of Schubert's winter traveller whose descent into insanity, if in an aeroplane, would have been caused by boredom or claustrophobia rather than a broken heart!). The Schubertian in you would approve of New Zealand – parts of it are as breath-taking and unspoiled as anything that inspired Franz and his poets to apostrophize the glories of Austrian hill, stream and lake. Of course, some aspects of the country may seem behind the times (no bad thing perhaps), and yet accompanists now are as well treated here as they are anywhere in the world, for you have educated people's attitudes far beyond the borders of the United Kingdom. Those of our profession who work in the Antipodes have reaped the benefits of your struggles, singers read your advice on the songs of Schubert and Schumann *et alia* and your gramophone record legacy is aired on the radio almost every day thanks to N.Z.'s excellent Concert Programme.

And so it is here that I have re-read *The Unashamed Accompanist* for the sixth or seventh time. And in doing so, the warmth and the open spaces of a land with a British inheritance remind me of my home country, now called Zimbabwe, where I first came across your indispensable manual. (For some years before that an African outpost of the Gerald Moore fan club had flourished in your absence. Your empire was built on shellac and later on long-playing plastic.) You did tell me once that you had visited my home town in 1929 over twenty years before I was born. I refuse, however, to feel it ridiculous that a song accompanist should have sprung from the colonies: I take enormous comfort in the fact that our greatly esteemed colleague Geoffrey Parsons is an Australian, and that you spent a good many of your formative years in Toronto.

I was eleven years old when I first read *The Unashamed Accompanist*; at that age, before you planted the seed, there was not a thought in my head that I might turn out to be an accompanist myself. I was simply an aspiring young pianist working my way through the grade examinations and local Rhodesian music festivals. I remember finding the book compulsive reading, even though the quotations of songs with tantalizing German gobbledegook underneath the music were beyond me, and the frequent mention of a man called Wolf (who never had any of his piano pieces set for Associated Board exams) puzzled me. I therefore classed him as a nonentity. You seemed such a nice man however, that I allowed you this passion for an unknown composer as a harmless eccentricity. I had certainly heard of Schubert, but I should point out that my first attempts at accompaniment as a ten year old (it was the D major Schubert violin Sonatina) proved such a musical débâcle that for some years the very name of that composer engendered feelings of panic within me, not to mention within my violinist colleague, her teacher and her mother. You on the other hand seemed to have such a lot of fun with Schubert. This was food for thought; music-making could be *fun*.

It was actually my wise piano teacher, Nora Hutchinson, who had given me the book as an antidote to my parents' worried theories that a career in music always meant a lonely life of endless solo engagements (fat chance!), which in the end caused a sort of bizarre eccentricity. (I have since discovered that people can become perfectly eccentric without having undertaken a single solo engagement in their lives!) The local music-shop owner authoritatively told my father that all the great solo pianists who had passed through Bulawayo were mad, or worse. Thinking now of how musical life in Bulawayo in those days must have struck these musical travellers I do not altogether blame them.

The Unashamed Accompanist was thus initially remarkable to my rather wary kin as a work-description by a man who had managed to make a living, playing the piano, without being either mad or lonely. This impressed them more as a virtuoso feat than all the pyrotechnical wizardry of Horowitz. The photographs of you in the book were also far too cosy and affable to depict a suffering spirit. Indeed for the guardians of a young boy who was increasingly endangered by the prospect of a life in music, eminent and reassuring sanity breathed from every page of the book. Even at that stage I gathered that the demands were great in the profession, that much hard work was required, but it was the sort of hard work that a reasonably ordinary and gregarious mortal could undertake without too much damage to his psyche. I must point out here however that it was to be some years before I encountered the challenges posed by the singing species. There were as many professional singers in Rhodesia as there are wild kangaroos in New Zealand; that is to say, absolutely none.

My parents were soothed by your tone (thousands have been in one way or another) and beguiled by your prose. Many years after encountering *The Unashamed Accompanist* in print, they met

you for themselves and could see that the open warmth and kindness writ large in the book were now a living and breathing example for their son, and a marvellous personal influence.

And that if I may say so is what is heartening about all your books, and of course about you. You have the gift of putting yourself into your writings exactly as you are, and the Un-ashamed Accompanist when encountered in the flesh is the same person as we have read about. With you, things are indeed as they seem. Your approval and disapproval (the latter always expressed with tact) are as clear as words on a printed page. We all know where we are with you. "My dear girl," you once said to a world-famous singer "I am certainly not going to play "An Silvia" at that ridiculously slow tempo and be the laughing-stock of London!" Would that we accompanists all had your courage, and what is even more important, the ability to say things like that with a twinkle in the eye and without giving offence.

Nouns like reality and honesty and phrases like "down-to-earth" and "feet-on-the-ground" (not even on the pedals?) can seem rather prosaic epithets of faint praise. But in the field of accompaniment they are great and shining virtues, to be taken even less for granted than pianistic flair or imaginative sensitivity. There is such a lot of glamour of the wrong sort in the music business, isn't there? And here there are other words which are alluring but also dangerous: money, fame, power and unreasonable ambition. The good accompanist's privilege is to work with people who are "stars" and who are inevitably acquainted with all these things in varying degree. How easy it is however to be led by these nightingales into a cloud-cuckoo land where music can become less important than the glittering prizes it can earn for the chosen few. I do believe that you have totally kept your independence from all this, and that you have been untouched by the "Hollywood" side of working with the great. You have re-fused to be subsumed into anyone's entourage. Of course you were ambitious for your profession and your place in it, but how different was your attitude from the sycophancy expected from and given by the lap-dog accompanists of the past.

To have kept a level head among the giants is the best sign of your own stature. As well as bringing errant artists down to size (when necessary for their good as well as yours) you were able to make giant occasions more human too. A friend of mine told me that he was at a Schwarzkopf/Moore recital at the Festival Hall (alas, before I had arrived in England) where the pre-concert atmosphere was thick with tension and electric expectation. I am sure both singer and pianist were nervous, the audience was on tenterhooks. If the first song had been, say, "Erlkönig" I am sure you would have used this tension to whip up even greater horror. The first item however was Schubert's "Der Einsame" in which, as you know well, a man contemplates his solitary but idyllic *modus vivendi* from the comfort of an armchair. In the piano part the crickets in the countryside chirp the friendly and companionable greetings. From the moment you began to play the piano it seemed for one listener at least (and probably for many more) that "all was right with the world", that the concert-goer could sit easily in his chair rather than on a knife-edge, that the singer was in safe hands, and the daunting impersonal spaces of the Festival Hall were shrunk into the warm domestic span of Schubert's fireside world. This was a perfect realization of what the song was about. It was as if Enid was in the next room getting the tea things ready, and I know for myself how comforting and heart-warming that feeling is! In a musical jungle of inflated expectations and egos (I wish I could also say fees, our fees that is!) you could defuse the unessential showbusiness aura surrounding an event and highlight the real and only important thing happening – the making of great music in a room of friends.

You have deflated me once or twice for my own good too. I shall never forget the end of your 80th birthday concert given by The Songmakers' Almanac at the Wigmore Hall in 1979. It had been a long concert and we were all very moved. Anthony Rolfe Johnson had ended the evening with an account of Strauss's "Freundliche Vision" which seemed to me so appropriate for you and Enid in your Buckinghamshire cottage:

> "As I walk
> With one who loves me
> Into the peace
> Of this white house."

When all the singing had stopped you came onto the platform and addressed the packed Wigmore Hall. You saluted the singing of Felicity Lott, Tony Rolfe Johnson and Richard Jackson in turn.

Graham Johnson with Ann Murray.

[119]

And then you came to me. "And as for the accompanist," you said benignly – and I hung my head with the modesty of one who expects kind words. I should have known better. With the comic genius of a man who could have made a living on the stage of the Palladium your face went momentarily blank. "As for the accompanist . . ." you stumbled, as if stuck for words – and then consulting your programme with furtive but immaculately-timed relish, you added your throwaway aside – "What was his name again?" Machiavelli Moore trouncing a young rival appeared for two seconds and it was a splendid pantomime for it teased and flattered me simultaneously. The audience howled with laughter, released at last from the solemnity of my programme-planning. You had provided a much needed antidote to an evening which threatened to become a little *too* moving. As always, your sense of proportion saved the day. This gift is a very English one (and I do think of you, born under the sign of Leo, as a very English somewhat Churchillian lion); if the accompanist's life is a question of "Am I too Loud?" then I say that the whole of your life has been a masterly management of balance in every sense of that word. It seems impossible by the way, that it should already be five years since you were last with all the Songmakers on that platform. Above the Wigmore stage there is a gilded (and possibly gelded) representation of an exotic and slim youth garlanded with leaves and wearing the saintly expression of an Apollonian Muse carried by his thoughts into the deeper realms of the spirit. I can never forget another occasion you stood under this stucco Ganymede, and pointing upwards said ruefully to the audience, "It has been some years since I modelled for that . . .".

Well anyway, you played Ganymede well as long as you stuck to songs by Schubert and Wolf which depict him truthfully! When we first met you still looked exactly the same as you do now, and I expect always did. I doubt if you remember that first meeting. You gave a master-class at the Royal Academy of Music in 1971. With a soprano, I performed Wolf's song "Er Ist's" which has a very trickly postlude. By then I knew a little more about Wolf than I did as a Rhodesian neophyte, but there was still a great deal I needed to know. You sat down to demonstrate. You could not know that this particular song would come up in the class, and I hope you will not mind me saying that you muffed it. Nearly everybody does, for it is a beast of a thing and it has been a source of pianistic humiliation on the concert platform for me on more than one occasion. At the beginning of the postlude's turbulence you shouted across to the singer, "For heaven's sake hold on to your last note, to cover this up!" So it was that you won my heart; the books and the man were as one in my mind from the start. Then there was a phase when you judged me in competitions rather a lot. On one occasion you called me over and said: "Mr Johnson, I'm not going to give you the award this time because I can't *go on* giving you prizes." You made me feel glad not to have won; it's little wonder that you have always had the power of making artists eat out of the hands which played for them.

In 1973 on leaving the R.A.M. I wrote to you for advice. What was I going to do with my career? May I remind you of how you replied? I sorted out some of your letters and brought them to New Zealand with me. Re-reading them has been a wonderful way of re-living the growth of our friendship:

5th January, 1973

Dear Mr Johnson,

If I had not heard you myself, Miss Flora Nielsen's enthusiasm for your work would have been enough in itself. But the only thing for you to do now is to sit tight. This is the experience that we all have to endure at some stage. I wonder if you would like to apply for the post of repetiteur at Glyndebourne? I would be glad to write on your behalf to Moran Caplat. If there is any other quarter where my influence might possibly be helpful let me know and I will write.

It was thus that the profession's most famous member greeted the newcomer. You somehow made me feel a colleague. I did sit tight and almost went to Glyndebourne. But I stayed with the song repertoire and two and a half years later organized a performance of Wolf's "Italienisches Liederbuch" in honour of the late Flora

[121]

Nielsen who was a dear friend to us both. From this concert sprang the idea of The Songmakers' Almanac, but not before you had taken me to task over the tempi of some of the Wolf songs in the measured tones of a reasonable scoutmaster. For I was now an enthusiastic Wolf cub and making up for all that lost time in Africa. The Almanac's first actual performance together, however, was at a concert of Mendelssohn and Schumann devised by you. For this Queen Elizabeth Hall performance in 1976, I persuaded you to play with me the piano duet accompaniment of Schumann's "Spanische Liebeslieder". Geoffrey Parsons said to me afterwards: "From the moment Gerald's hands touched the keys, we could hear that special sound of his. There is nothing like it." I also remember Walter Legge often saying that your sound was due to your cushioned finger pads which made every note you played as succulent as a fat, juicy oyster. Even my playing of the "secondo" part and my pedalling could not obscure your unique sonority on that very last occasion that we were lucky enough to hear you on the South Bank.

Right from the Almanac's beginning you were a Patron. You became deeply interested in the careers of all four singers who were founder members. Three of them took part in your 80th birthday concert, and Ann Murray you had known and admired since hearing her in Barcelona long before the Almanac was formed. In the days when you came to concerts in town regularly we had the keenest ears in the business working on our behalf. Here is just one example of the "notice" I received from Buckinghamshire, more feared and attended to than the praises or whippings of the press.

7th August, 1978

Dear Graham,

I listened with all my ears to Schubert's second "Suleika" song, for I have always felt, when playing it, I was on a tightrope. The opening tempo is marked "Mässige Bewegung" (with moderate movement), then later comes "Etwas geschwinder" – (somewhat faster,) and this "Etwas" of yours was an express train. I found it too fast (at least for

the Wigmore) for surely the essence of this section is the
bouncing repeated notes which lost character at this speed.

What we mostly heard was ♩♪ ♩♪ instead of ♫♪ ♫♪
I always abandoned the sustaining pedal here.

Thanks to you I will (hopefully) play that song with greater
understanding and more judicious tempi. You were right as
always. And everything I've ever asked you to listen to, whether
concert, broadcast or gramophone record, has received the same
frank appraisal. In December 1979 you wrote:

> It gives us a feeling of pride that you have "adopted" us (or
> is it vice-versa?) for we have not only a great affection for
> you but a pride in your accomplishments. For this reason
> (this pride) it seems very unfeeling or insensitive on my part
> to make these criticisms from time to time. (You must
> forgive an old boy's relish when he feels he can seize on
> something which he hopes will be constructive.)

Forgiveness has nothing to do with it Gerald, for I have had the
glorious privilege of having a *living* volume of the Unashamed
Accompanist on my side and by the phone. I feel as if you wrote
the book for me (but then so does every accompanist) and that
you have carefully and conscientiously followed up the flowerings
of the the seeds the book planted in my life over twenty years ago.
I know too that even without the personal touch which has been
my great good fortune, your book has had a potent influence on
thousands of pianists who never met you. Only the other day for
example, in a *New York Times* article I saw your name gratefully
invoked by our American colleague Samuel Sanders. After all
these years there is nothing dated in *The Unashamed Accompanist*,
and it remains as succinct a summing up of the art of accompaniment that is ever likely to be written. All your explanations and
analyses of the skills we need to develop are exactly right, but the
unabashed title of the book is the key to the mental attitude we
must all possess in order to practise these skills with authority, with
belief in ourselves. In some ways your book is a political manifesto.
It encourages us to be proud of our profession and to be angry

about the abuse of the "mere accompanist" – an epithet used by a *Times* critic not many years ago, in comparing a solo pianist's accompanying with the work of full-time accompanists. You took issue with this reference in the letter columns of that paper, (we all admire the solo pianist in question but that was not the point) and the critic apologized. All us "mere" accompanists had once more to thank you as our champion.

I was working very recently on writing a programme about Brahms and came across an incident recounted in the Specht biography of that composer. The story was meant to be delightful and charming but it made me angry because there was a forgotten and unmentioned person in it, namely the "mere" as opposed to the "celebrity" accompanist. Towards the end of his life Johannes Brahms accompanied the mezzo-soprano Alice Barbi at a concert in Vienna. It was taken to be a sign of his mute and adoring devotion to her that he appeared at the last minute and without warning to play the accompaniments. Let us not ask how good this recital was without any preparation or rehearsal. (We know only too well that love and empathy do not make for automatic perfect ensemble, and we also know for a fact that at this time of his life Brahms was prone to play a lot of wrong notes and puff and grunt while he played them.) Let us ask rather what happened to the poor wretch who had been expecting to accompany Barbi's recital? The answer is that the composer arrived and swept him aside much to the admiration and applause of the deeply moved and celebrity-hungry audience. And no doubt the accompanist being ever the figure of humble understanding (for some reason we are classed as perpetual students who are considered lucky to get "the experience" well into old age) was also deeply moved to see his night's work evaporate before his eyes. Did he get his fee I wonder? I couldn't help thinking when I read this, that this was more or less the state of the profession when you entered it as a young man. One shudders to think of the subtle and less subtle indignities inflicted on your forbears, and my grand-forbears as it were, fine artists like George Reeves, Conrad V. Bos, Paula Hegner, Harold Craxton and many other unsinging and unsung heroes. There have even been times in your career when it has been a singer's choice that conductors, even solo pianists (if not actually composers) should usurp your place at the keyboard to the appreciative oohs-and-aahs of the public. Many of these luminaries singularly failed (as is immediately audible to anyone who knows the music from the inside) to play accurately or even together with their artists. But then one of the great advantages of coming from a "humble" (and I would prefer to say realistic) background is that we can survive the competition of publicity-conscious pairings when the needs of the music are not considered first. We know that good, honest performances of the music are all that matters. We do not often play for the high financial or prestige stakes of some of our collaborator colleagues, though there is a possibility that we may have a longer and surer career. Instead, we have the dignity of fulfilling a unique role in which we can afford to be disinterested in the best sense. It is you who have once and for all defined that role, and provided an enduring example of how to be a witty and urbane observer of musical life and its absurdities. But disinterest and a sense of proportion do not mean coldness and lack of interest. You love music and music-making far too much to be tempted into the cynicism which can be the accompanist's occupational hazard if he allows himself to be downtrodden.

And so, dear Gerald, it is now the year of your 85th birthday. No accompanist before you has achieved such world-wide celebrity, and it is a fairly safe bet that no one accompanist of the future will dominate the profession in the same way. London in the great days of the recording industry was a heady place. You were in the right place at the right time to reach your unique position. More important than time or place however was that you were the right man with the right musical and personal qualifications to change the history of accompaniment once and for all. Any accompanist coming after you will have to say to him or herself, "Can I have a career?" In effect, "Am I, too, allowed?" And the answer will be: "Perhaps, but never in the same way." You say it all in the very last paragraph of the book, it's the heart that matters and hearts are made one at a time, and not too often like yours. And so bless that heart of yours, your bright toughness, your wicked humour and your wonderful wife who is so strongly woven into the fabric of your life and success that all who know and value you think of you both in the same breath of affection. I know you could never have played the same without her accompaniment. From New Zealand I send love to you both, and I know how much you (not Enid!) would love to be here in Wellington's rain and sunshine to watch the forthcoming Test match. No singer I suspect was ever as much of a hero to you as a great cricketer. With such steadfast Englishry in your blood, no wonder other nations could never field a rival capable of chalking up so many runs. And you did all yours sitting down at the keyboard!

Your devoted

GRAHAM